"A hilariously funny send-up of any and every spy story you care to name from OUR MAN IN HAVANA to GOLDFINGER."

—Peter George
Co-author of DR. STRANGELOVE

"An entertainment of high order."

—Capital Times

"A real sparkler of spoofery. . . . Excellent fun all the way."

—Saturday Review

"Hilarious, from the first page through the torture chamber of the Doges in Venice to the climax in an Alpine hunting lodge."

—St. Louis Post-Dispatch

ROBERT SHECKLEY

A DIVISION OF CHARTER COMMUNICATIONS INC.
A GROSSET & DUNLAP COMPANY

TO ZIVA

THE GAME OF X

A Charter Book published by arrangement with Dell Publishing Co., Inc.

First Charter Printing September 1980
Published simultaneously in Canada
Manufactured in the United States of America

2 4 6 8 0 9 7 5 3 1

THE GAME OF X

1

It had been a long, hard day. My appointments had been spread all over Paris; near the Opéra, across the river to Vanves, then back to the Faubourg St. Honoré, then back to the Opera. Results: nothing.

It was close to seven when I dragged myself out of the Metro at the Cluny stop. It was April in Paris; an endless line of Diesel trucks barreled down the Boulevard St. Michel. A cold and hopeless rain was falling. I was tired, footsore and frustrated. My mouth hurt from talking French to sullen receptionists. I wanted to go back to my room and boil an egg. But I had promised to meet George for a drink.

He was waiting for me in an ugly little cafe near the École. We talked for a while about the weather. At last he asked me if I had found a job yet, and I told him I hadn't. He became very thoughtful.

I have known George since high-school days,

but we have very little in common. George is squat, purposive, and exceedingly practical. I am tall, unmotivated, and inclined to dubious speculations. George had come to Europe to fill a minor technical position in an obscure government agency. I had not waited for a specific invitation.

Being prepared to hold any job, I was offered none. I soon found that there was no future, nor even much of a present, in selling the Paris edition of the *Herald Tribune*. I did chauffeur (illegally, for scab wages) a gleaming Buick from Le Havre to Paris. And once I found a job playing bass with a French jazz combo in Montmartre. But in order to work with them I had to have a permit, for which I applied at the Services de Main d'Oeuvre du Ministère du Travail. I was turned down, since my employment would rob some deserving French bass player of the opportunity.

I was discouraged but not embittered. I liked Europe and wanted to stay. I wanted to live in an apartment in Rome, with icy marble floors, inadequate heating, no refrigerator, a loggia, a patio, French windows, a balcony, and a view of the Borghese Gardens. In a pinch I was even willing to forgo the loggia.

But alas, this modest goal seemed forever beyond my reach. My funds had come down to the vanishing point; with the last of them, I too would be forced to disappear.

"I might have work for you," George said, after considerable thought.

"Indeed?" I replied.

George looked around. We were completely

alone except for three hundred students. Lowering his voice, he said, "Bill, how would you like to help trap a spy?"

"Sure," I said. "I'd be glad to."

"I'm quite serious about this."

"I realize that," I said. "I'm serious, too. Will I get a chance to wear a trench coat and carry a gun in a shoulder holster?"

"No guns," George said.

"Will I at least be working with a lovely mysterious lady?"

"Not even that."

"You don't make it sound very interesting," I told him. "Maybe I should offer my services to MI-5 or the Sûreté."

"Listen to me," George said angrily. "It's no joke."

I started to grin, then stopped. In the fifteen years I had known George, he had made very few jokes, and none like this.

"I really think you mean it," I said.

"Yes, I really do."

I sat and stared at him. I had always wondered how one became a secret agent. Now I knew; one was asked into the business by a friend who was already in the business.

"Well?" George said after a while.

"Well what?"

"Are you interested?"

"I told you I was. When do I start?"

"I wish," George said sternly, "that you would think for a moment before making your decision."

So I thought, just to please him. I considered my qualifications for the adventurous life of secret agent. I could fire an M-1 rifle with reasonable accuracy, and drive a sports car at modest speeds. I had helped sail a Hereshoff S-boat from Manhasset to Port Jefferson, and had once handled the controls of a Piper Cub. I could speak broken French, Spanish and Italian, and had taken three hours of instruction in judo. And, of course, I had read extensively about all aspects of the Vigorous Life in the pages of many now-defunct pulp magazines. In brief, I was as well prepared as the next man.

I also thought about how interesting this job could be, and how very little money I had, and how poor my job prospects were in Paris, and how I had no intention of returning to the States. I knew that George was serious, and even feeling a little grim about the whole thing; but I just couldn't get into an appropriate mood. I had always heard that Europe was filled with secret agents of all nationalities, sexes, sizes, shapes and colors; but the thought of George or me in that kind of work seemed ludicrous.

"All right," I said. "I've thought about it."

"You seem to be having a very curious reaction," George said coldly. I think I had offended his dignity.

"Sorry," I said. "I am trying to accustom myself to the idea. How long have you worked for the CIA?"

"I work for an autonomous organization. We cooperate with CIA, of course."

"And why did you ask me? I mean, isn't this sort of work kept inside the organization?"

"It usually is. But we need someone who's had no previous connection with us, or with CIA or any of the others."

"Why?"

"In order to trap a spy," George said, "one should use fresh bait."

That sounded the least bit unpleasant; but I couldn't blame him.

"Also," he added, "we had to have someone of the right age and appearance, whom we could trust. You are my oldest friend, and I trust you absolutely."

"Thank you," I said.

"Well, then, if you're still sure, let's go speak to my chief. He'll fill you in on the details."

George paid for the drinks. As we started to leave, he added, "You mustn't expect a great deal of money, by the way. We're tightly budgeted and it's only a brief assignment."

"I had expected nothing more than to serve," I told him. Perhaps I was insufferably breezy, but that was because George was so incredibly stuffy.

We went to George's office on the Boulevard Haussmann. There I was interviewed by a Colonel Baker. He was a small, neat, khaki-skinned man with steel-colored eyes and an ironic little mouth. His fingernails were badly chewed; I liked him very much.

The situation was explained to me. It concerned a certain Anton Karinovsky, a Roumanian by birth, a Russian agent by occupation. This man, under various names and disguises, had been making a nuisance of himself in Western Europe for some years. Colonel Baker had been given the task of doing something about it.

There had followed a long period of paperwork, surveillance, and just plain waiting. At last Baker's organization had identified, with reasonable certainty, a man whom they believed to be Karinovsky.

Some heavy planning followed, and then some fancy footwork, and after that a little sleight-of-hand. It had all culminated in a Scheme, known technically as an Entrapment. In two days, Karinovsky would be taking a train to Barcelona. I was to be with him on that train. I was the Bait; in the quaint jargon of the Service, I was known as the Cheese.

"It's all right with me," I said. "But I'd better warn you. I haven't handled a firearm since I graduated from the service."

Baker grimaced. "Didn't George tell you? No guns."

"He did mention that, and it's OK with me. But will Karinovsky follow our rules?"

"There will be no violence," Baker said. "All you must do is follow orders."

"To hear is to obey," I replied. And wheels began to turn.

Twenty-four hours later, a certain one-star American General on vacation in Pamplona received an urgent request from the two-star commander of the U.S. 22nd Armored stationed in Sangüesa. The General made a hurried search of his papers, came to an embarrassing realization, and fired off a coded telegram to his office in Paris. Shortly after receipt of his telegram, a certain civilian made a visit to Third Army Headquarters on the Avenue de Neuilly. There, in an office on the second floor, a frowning Colonel handed this personable young fellow a briefcase.

The young man sauntered out of the building, looked around casually on all sides, and hailed a taxi. He was wearing a Madras sports shirt, Daks, an Italian silk jacket, and highly polished Scotch Grain brogues. Only his handkerchief, of an olive-gray GI hue, was not of impeccable civilian origin.

The personable young chap was myself, smack in the middle of Colonel Baker's Byzantine intrigue. I was supposed to be carrying some papers in an inobtrusive manner to my red-faced General. Also, I was supposed to be looking like a man who was trying *not* to look like an American military attaché, a difficult bit of characterization. How Karinovsky was supposed to learn all of this was frankly beyond my comprehension. I considered the whole affair hopelessly complicated. Of course, I knew nothing of the tortuous ways of spies. And in any event, Baker had told me not to worry about it.

I arrived at the Gare Lyon and soon thereafter I was in a first-class compartment on the Sud Express, holiday-bound for Pamplona and the annual running of the gringos. The Cheese was on the move; and, amazingly enough, the Mouse was close behind.

I didn't have to look for Karinovsky; he found me, as had been anticipated. We had the compartment to ourselves. Karinovsky was a middle-aged man with a tough, square face, a dark moustache, heavy, pouched eyes, a busted nose, clipped gray hair, and big ears. He could have been a defensive linebacker, or a Hungarian infantry colonel, or even a Sicilian bandit. He said he was a Swiss watch salesman named Schoner. I said I was an assistant travel-agency manager named Lymington.

We talked. Or rather, Karinovsky talked. He was a soccer fanatic, and he went on endlessly about Switzerland's chances in the forthcoming match with Milan. We smoked the air blue, my Chesterfields losing out to his Gauloises. Onward we plunged through the green French countryside. By the time we reached Vichy, he had exhausted soccer and switched to Grand Prix racing. My eyes glazed at the flash and roar of Ferraris, Aston-Martins, Alfa-Romeos and Lotuses. I went through a pack of cigarettes in two hours, and started another. It was warm in the compartment. I mopped my forehead with the telltale khaki handkerchief, and thought I saw a feral gleam in Karinovsky's muddly little eyes. But there was no break in his monologue. The man was unstoppable. My bladder was near to bursting (an occupational hazard of spies, I learned later), and my mouth tasted like an ossuary. I think we were somewhere around Périgueux when he started to tell me about his life and times as a watch salesman. He was literally boring me to death. My nerves were worn to the quick by his dry, flat, rasping voice, and my mind was numbed by an avalanche of sports information, spurious opinions, and utterly predictable anecdotes.

I had a dangerous desire to shock him into silence. Instead, I excused myself and went to the john. I took my briefcase with me and returned in less than five minutes. Sure as death, we continued our conversation. But now, finally, the train was slowing down for the border inspection at Hendaye.

Karinovsky was slowing down, too. He began to chew his moustache. He looked suddenly mottled around the gills. He said he was feeling distinctly unwell, and I went for the conductor. When I returned, Karinovsky was slumped over holding his stomach. He seemed to have fever. The conductor and I began to speculate on appendicitis.

We helped him off the train at Hendaye. When we started again, I checked my briefcase. I saw at once that it was not mine, though the resemblance was uncanny. Karinovsky must have switched briefcases while I had gone off for the conductor. The one he had given me contained newspapers. The one he had taken from me had held a military progress report bearing a "Restricted" classification. The briefcase had also contained one thousand dollars in travelers' checks. So far, everything was going according to plan.

I rode the train one stop farther, to Massat. There I got off, went into a cafe called the Blue Moose, and waited for a telephone call. I waited three hours, and no call came for me. I caught the next train back to Paris and bought myself a very good dinner.

The next day I reported to Colonel Baker's office. The Colonel and George were positively overflowing with good spirits. Baker opened a bottle of champagne and told me what had happened.

He and George and one or two others had

been waiting at the Hendaye station when Karinovsky got off. Politely but firmly they had wedged Karinovsky into a quiet cafe and spelled out the facts of life for him. To wit:

Karinovsky had stolen a briefcase containing an important military document, plus the sum of one thousand American dollars. The briefcase was easily identifiable; witnesses were available; and the owner of the briefcase was waiting in Massat, prepared to swear out a complaint and to pursue it to the fullest extent of French law. It should mean at least ten years in a French prison.

Karinovsky knew a bear-trap when he saw one. He had been tricked and trapped. He was ready to talk business.

Terms were discussed over the next half hour. Baker didn't tell me what they were, but apparently he had found them satisfactory. The case was closed.

Then George said, "But of course, you haven't heard the best of it."

"I wonder if we should tell him," Baker mused.

"Why not, sir?" George asked. "After all, he was involved in this."

"I suppose so," Baker said. He leaned back in his armchair. A reminiscent twinkle came into his kindly gimlet eyes. "Well, it happened in the cafe, just after Karinovsky realized how much trouble he was in. He was thinking furiously, trying to figure out where he had gone wrong, and why, and how, and who had trapped him so neatly. He thought for quite a while, and then he looked up with an expression of growing horror on his face. He said, 'Christ! That stupid military fellow on the train was in on it, wasn't he?' "

Baker had smiled and said, "Are you referring to our Mr. Nye?"

Karinovsky's shoulders had slumped. He said, "I should have guessed. Obviously, that idiot is in your employment."

"Not exactly," Baker said, in a sudden flash of inspiration. "You might more correctly say that *we* are in the employment of that idiot."

Karinovsky had gaped. "I do not believe you," he said. But it was obvious that he did.

Then Baker knew that he had created an interesting illusion in Karinovsky's mind. He had conjured up the image of a paragon of agents, of awesome intellectual powers and highly developed skills.

Always a pragmatist, Baker had accepted this unexpected windfall. He dealt in illusions, after all; it seemed to him that this one might prove useful if Karinovsky ever balked. Individuation, in the final analysis, was everything; accordingly, it was much more impressive to have the specter of Secret Agent Nye peering over Karinovsky's shoulder rather than some faceless organization. And, beyond this purely practical consideration, other possibilities glimmered like marsh fire: a shadow agent can undertake much more dangerous assignments than his fleshy counterparts. A specter is not susceptible to capture by normal methods.

Yes, there was work for Agent X—as Baker had already begun to think of him. Agent X utilized that law of human nature which makes con men the easiest victims of a con game. The law of autopredation, Baker decided to call it; the iron rule by which an inevitably merciful Nature turns the specialized strength of the predator into a fatal weakness, and thus betrays a vested interest in long-range averages.

So it seemed to Baker, flushed with the intoxication of success and believing, for the moment, that nothing was beyond his grasp. One word from him and phantom armies marched, and men of blood shuddered at their advance.

In a kindly voice he had said to Karinovsky, "Our Mr. Nye took you in, did he?"

"I used to consider myself a judge of men," Karinovsky said. "And I could have sworn that this man was a nothing—a nonentity—a thoroughly negligible person, and surely not a professional."

"Nye's always been good at giving that impression," Baker said. "It's one of his little specialties."

"If what you tell me is true," Karinovsky said, "then the man is a formidable operative. But of course, you planned out the details of this operation yourself?"

Baker thought about the long months of dull routine, the superb coordination of his team of agents, and his own brilliance in producing a scheme tailored for Karinovsky and none other. He wanted to tell Karinovsky about it. But he didn't. He sacrificed a moment of petty gloating in the interests of his new illusion.

"I wish I *had* planned it," Baker said. "But the truth is, I disapproved of the plan from the start. I didn't think it would work. But Nye overruled me. And, as usual, he was right."

Baker had smiled bitterly. "One cannot argue with success, can one?"

"No," Karinovsky had agreed, "one cannot." He sighed deeply.

And that was that. We opened a second bottle of champagne and drank a toast to success. George asked me how it felt to be an ultra-special agent, and I told him it felt fine, which it did. Colonel Baker, musing pleasurably on his invention, said that he had always wanted to create his very own operative. The real ones were barely able to find their way home in the dark. He told me several amusing stories to illustrate the point.

We parted soon after that. I had a plain white envelope in my pocket. It contained five hundred dollars, which I considered a very adequate reward for a day's work.

It had been a pleasant affair. Of course, I assumed at the time that that was the end of it.

2

The next few weeks were an inconclusive sort of time for me. I tended bar (illegally) for several weekends in a *boîte* near the Place des Vosges. I loafed and invited my soul on the banks of the Seine, also on the Ile Saint-Louis, also in the gloomy little garden behind Saint-Germain-des-Prés. I discovered a cache of Air-War pulps in a bookstore on the Rue de la Huchette, read voraciously, and considered doing an essay on the Age of Aerial Innocence. But I didn't. Instead I applied for a job as consulting editor of a new French science-fiction magazine, was accepted, and then saw the whole thing fall through when the prospective publisher ran out of money.

Thus, my position was essentially unchanged when I received a call from George about six weeks after *l'affair* Karinovsky. It seemed that Colonel Baker wanted to see me. I went at once. Our last transaction had been more than satisfactory. I don't know what secret agents normally earn; but, at Baker's rates, I was definitely interested in continuing my new career.

The Colonel came to the point at once. "It's about that fellow you brought in last month," he said.

I thought it very decent of the Colonel to phrase it that way.

"What about him?" I asked.

"He wants to come over."

"That's a surprising development," I said.

"Not particularly. Karinovsky is a professional. As such, he is likely to change sides when offered the proper inducement."

"I see," I said.

"You probably understood," Baker told me, "that I came to an arrangement with Karinovsky last month. I wanted certain information, which he supplied. This, of course, gave me a further hold over him. After that, I wanted more information. And more, and more. I was insatiable." He smiled a nasty little smile. "It put Karinovsky into the position of a double agent; potentially, a very dangerous situation. It was only a matter of time before his people found out. Now he wants to come over, which is something of a coup for us."

I said, "Well, sir, that's very good news."

"But of course, it isn't quite as simple as that. The thing must be arranged with care, and an agent must be assigned to control the operation and render physical assistance if necessary. In this case, Karinovsky has requested the aid of a specific agent. You."

"Me, sir?"

"Yes, you. Specifically and exclusively you. It is, I suppose, a predictable consequence of our little deception. Karinovsky is in Venice at present, and he needs to get out rather urgently. He wants help from our best man—the redoubtable Agent X. He not only wants it, he expects it. Under the circumstances, I would dislike having to tell him that Agent X is a figment of our imagination."

"There's no reason to tell him," I said. "I am quite prepared to render whatever assistance is necessary."

"That's very good of you," Baker said. "I was hoping you would say that. But I think I should mention that there is a certain irreducible element of danger in this assignment. Not too much, I believe; but it cannot be discounted."

"That doesn't alarm me, sir."

The Colonel looked considerably cheered. "Actually, it's simple enough. Karinovsky is in Venice. He has already been in contact with our resident agent, Marcantonio Guesci. All you'll have to do, really, is fly down to Venice and get in touch with Guesci. He'll arrange everything, and spirit both you and Karinovsky out of Italy. The entire operation should take no more than a day or two. You would merely have to follow Guesci's instructions."

I was a little disappointed at hearing this. The Colonel evidently planned to use me as nothing more than a figurehead, a sort of imitation of a secret agent. Of course, I hadn't expected to be in charge of the case this early in my career; but still, I had hoped for a little more responsibility.

"It's all right with me," I said.

"Excellent," Colonel Baker said. "I would

prefer, by the way, to keep your true identity a secret. Not even Guesci need know the truth about Agent X. I mean, I have full confidence in your abilities, but Guesci might not."

"What if Guesci wants to talk shop?" I asked.

"He won't. But in case he does, our story is that you've just been transferred from Far East Command. No one around here knows what those fellows do. I doubt if they know themselves."

"All right," I said.

"It's really quite simple," Baker said, for the second time. "The only complicating factor is Karinovsky's former employers. They won't want to let Karinovsky slip away; that sort of thing lowers morale and looks very bad on the records."

"What will they do?"

"Try to kill him, I suppose. We want to prevent that."

"Yes, sir. How many of them are there?"

"Six or eight, I suppose. You'll study the dossiers before you go. They're a ham-handed bunch for the most part. Except for Forster."

"Sir?"

"Forster is head of Soviet Intelligence Operations, Northeast Italian sector. He's a formidable fellow, a big, powerful chap, skilled with small arms and quite ingenious at planning. Definitely a man on his way up. But I suspect that he's overconfident."

"How am I supposed to handle him?"

The Colonel thought about that for a while. At last he said, "I think the best plan would be to avoid him entirely."

That didn't sound too promising. Forster

seemed to have a fearsome reputation. But then, I had a fearsome reputation, too. His deeds might well be as insubstantial as mine; anything was possible in this line of work. And frankly, the element of danger was intriguing rather than dismaying. It was difficult to become frightened in a snug office on the Boulevard Haussmann; but it was easy to dream of Venice, of the pigeons wheeling over the Piazza San Marco, and the motorboats racing down the Grand Canal, and myself walking into Doney's with money in my pocket. . . .

Colonel Baker and I had a short, interesting discussion on the subject of money. I finally accepted the sum of fifteen hundred dollars for what should be no more than two days' work. I thought that I was doing very well. I even felt a little embarrassed at taking such a large sum for such an easy assignment.

I was very busy for the next forty-eight hours, studying dossiers, poring over maps of Venice, and soaking up the necessary background. Then Baker got word from Guesci. Karinovsky had gone into hiding, and the escape route was ready. The next morning I was on an airplane to Venice.

3

My airplane touched down at Venice's Aeroporto Marco Polo at 11:30 in the morning. I cleared customs and passport control without difficulty, and walked out of the airport building.

It was a warm and lucid day. Directly ahead of me was the pier, crowded with boatmen offering their assorted craft for the short journey across the lagoon to the Piazza San Marco. Across the gleaming water I could see Venice itself, presenting its incredible skyline of sagging spires and tilted rectangular towers, pinnacles and chimneys, humpbacked buildings and crenellated walls.

My first reaction was literary and spurious; I thought of Atlantis, Port-Royal, and Ys of Armorica. Then I took notice of the huge grain elevator, and I saw how the fairy silhouettes were bound together by a tracery of power lines and television aerials. The city now seemed a fraud, a clumsy and willful anachronism. But that wasn't the truth, either.

This double effect was uniquely Venetian. The city has always been too stunning and too meretricious, and much too demanding of raw appreciation. When you see the Serenissima admiring herself in her mirror of dirty water, you are inevitably annoyed. But, however much you may deplore the lady's conceits, honesty forces you to admit her charms.

I wanted to go to her at once; but my instructions were to proceed first to the mainland city of Mestre, there to meet Guesci and discuss strategy. I turned regretfully to the west, where a great oily pall of smoke marked my immediate destination.

A green and black Fiat pulled up, driven by a smiling, glossy-haired young man wearing amber shades.

"How much to the Excelsior in Mestre?" I asked him.

"Sir, I will make you a very good price—"

Then I was shouldered aside. A fat man with a fat camera, wearing a blond business suit and a hand-painted necktie, with a porter behind him carrying two leather bags of expensive appearance, pushed past me.

"Take me to Mestre," he said, "and make it snappy." His strident tones and flat vowels identified him as a countryman of mine.

"This taxi is already occupied," the driver said.

"Like hell it is," the fat man said, easing himself through the doorway like a maggot entering a wound.

"It is occupied," the driver said again.

The fat man noticed me for the first time. He decided to be charming. "You don't mind, do you? I'm really in one hell of a hurry."

I did mind, but not very much. "Help yourself," I said, and started to pull my B-4 bag away.

But my glossy young driver shook his head firmly and put a restraining hand on my wrist. "No," he said, "you have hired me."

"Look, he said it was OK," the fat man said.

"But *I* have not said it was OK," the driver told him. He was not smiling now. He was a nervous little fellow, and his sensibilities had been outraged. I hadn't received any instructions about taxis, but at this point I wouldn't have ridden across the street with him without an armed escort. Call it a premonition.

The fat man had made himself comfortable on the back seat. He wiped his forehead and said to the driver, "Look, stop being ridiculous, let's roll."

"We shall not roll," the driver said. It looked as if the one big moment of his day had been the thought of driving me into Mestre. And now the fat man had robbed him of the pleasure.

"Get going," the fat man said, "or I'll call a cop."

"On the contrary," the driver said, "it is I who will call a policeman if you do not exit yourself on the instant."

"So call," the fat man said complacently. He winked at me: damned uppity, these natives.

Another taxi came up, and I started toward it. For a moment the glossy young man tightened his hand on my wrist; but at the last moment he must have recognized the inevitability of losing my company. He let go and gave me a what-friends-we-might-have-been look. Then he folded his arms and leaned back against his fender.

I got into the second cab. As we moved into the main road, I looked back and saw that the fat man was shouting angrily at the driver, who was still slouched against the fender. No other taxi was in sight.

My new driver was a middle-aged man with an engaging monkey face. He drove his little Fiat with considerable dash, and he kept up a ceaseless conversation. It gave me a chance to air my cover story.

"First time in Venice?"

"No, I was here once before."

"Ah! You are tourist?"

"Sales representative."

"Ah, that is why you go to Mestre?"

"Yes."

"What do you sell?"

"Business machines."

"Business machines? Like typewriters? Ah, you are a salesman of typewriters. And this brings you all the way from America?"

"That's about it," I told him. My cover story was getting an unexpected workout.

"You must sell many typewriters," the driver said.

"Enough."

"Do you sell more than Olivetti?"

"No. But we're trying."

"The Olivetti is a superb machine," the driver

stated dogmatically. "My niece, who works for a lawyer, has told me so."

"Mmmm," I said.

"What is the name of your machine?"

"Adams-Finetti."

"I have never heard of it."

"We're really better known for our adding machines," I told him.

The driver stopped asking questions and concentrated on racing a trolley across an intersection. He beat it, and opened up for a straightaway. A 2 CV came up on his left, and a promising unknown in an Alfa-Romeo took position on his right. Just behind us, a supercharged Bentley with triple stacks and lowered suspension was waiting to make its bid.

My driver jammed the accelerator to the floor and swerved superbly around fixed obstacles such as old ladies, baby carriages, and pushcarts. I leaned back with ersatz calm.

We held our lead through a tunnel. The 2 CV, obviously outclassed, fell back. The Bentley, its great pipes bellowing, made its bid. But my driver swung into the center of the road, matching his skill against his opponent's greater horsepower. He began to sing, just as the late great Pastafazu had been known to sing during the stickier moments at Le Mans.

Now a motorcycle pulled up beside us. It rode parallel to my window, and for a moment the driver and I were staring at each other. He was clad in Early Brando; black leather pants and jacket, glass-studded kidney belt, gauntlets, Wellington boots and crash helmet. No face; just fur-rimmed goggles and a mouth. He was driving a big, high-powered Indian.

We looked at each other for a while. Then he twisted the throttle and shot ahead of us, disappearing into the stream of traffic.

A lot of people seemed to be interested in me. I tried to tell myself that nobody could be on to me this soon.

We came into the outskirts of Mestre and the driver turned abruptly into a narrow, tenement-lined street. I frowned and sat up. The driver grinned at me and increased speed.

We shot past garages and stores. Everything seemed to be closed; even the sidewalks were deserted. I imagined the people hidden behind their heavy wooden shutters, waiting for a seasonal violence to erupt in their sun-blasted streets. A faint preliminary edge of panic touched me: the accelerating car, the empty noontime streets, the fat man, the taxi driver, the cyclist.

My driver abruptly slammed on his brakes and wrestled the taxi to a stop in the middle of the street. Two men ran out of doorways on either side and got into the cab beside me. The driver stamped his foot on the accelerator, and we started moving fast again.

4

The man on my left was sportily clad in chocolate slacks, beige sports shirt, raw silk jacket, alligator shoes, and walnut-handled .38 revolver. He nudged me in the side with the gun, like a kid playing stick-'em-up. He had a narrow, nasty little face and a pointy moustache.

"Take care," he said. "No sudden moves, no shoutings. Right?"

"Right," I said.

"Observe," he said, flipping out the cylinder of his revolver. "Fully loaded." He closed the cylinder. "Safety is off, gun set to fire on double-action. Right?"

"Right," I said.

"Beppo," he said to his pal on my right, "show him your gun."

"Never mind," I said, "I believe you."

"Why should you believe me?" the man asked. "Maybe I'm lying. Beppo, show him."

Beppo was a sour-faced man of imposing

build. He took his gun out of my kidneys, opened it, waited until I nodded, then closed it again.

"That's a great routine you boys have," I said.

"We are glad you like it, Mr. Nye," said the dude on my left. "You may call me Carlo."

"Because it's not your name?" I asked, feeling lightheaded.

"Correct," Carlo said, beaming.

"Is he also part of your act?" I asked, pointing at the driver.

"He's a humorist, too," Carlo said. "Aren't you, Giovanni?"

"I know some very funny stories," the driver said. "Listen, have you ever heard about the two priests and the well-digger's daughter?"

"I've heard it," Beppo growled. "When will you learn some new stories?"

Carlo laughed, and I joined in. I was feeling slightly hysterical. I had recognized their faces from Colonel Baker's dossiers. Which meant that I was in trouble.

"Well, well," Carlo said, wiping his eyes, still chuckling. "Here we are."

The taxi turned into an alley, twisted into a courtyard, went around a dry concrete fountain, and then squeezed into another courtyard. Giovanni stopped the car and we all got out.

On three sides there were crumbling brick walls and boarded-up windows. On the fourth side there was a bicycle repair shop on the ground floor. The upper two stories had French windows and narrow balconies.

"We are home," Carlo said. He clicked on the safety and put his revolver away in a chamois holster under his left arm. Beppo kept his revolver in his fist.

"This way," Beppo said. He took me by the arm.

The moment he touched me, I yanked my arm free and started to run.

Carlo had already moved between me and the exit. He had his gun out. He said, "Stop, or I will shoot out your right kneecap."

That was a pretty sobering thought. I stopped.

"Put your hands behind your head," Carlo said. I did so. Carlo stepped up, snarled something, and raked me across the forehead with the front gunsight.

I heard the sound of someone clapping. We all looked up.

One of the French windows was open. A man stood on the little balcony. He clapped three times; the contemptuous applause echoed against the brick walls.

"Strange," he said in a conversational voice, "how, for some men, the possession of a gun acts as a powerful intoxicant. It destroys the reasoning faculties, eh, Carlo?"

"He was trying to escape," Carlo said.

"But I specifically told you not to damage the merchandise," the man said gently. "Men with guns must learn not to shoot their livelihood."

"I'm sorry, Mr. Forster," Carlo said.

The man on the balcony nodded. He said, "Do come inside, Mr. Nye. We can discuss our business at leisure."

Forster turned and left the balcony. Carlo and Beppo closed on either side of me. They led me into the bicycle shop. The driver had taken a rag out of his pocket and was polishing the hood of his cab.

5

"Welcome to sunny Italy," Forster said.

"Awfully nice to be here," I replied. But I was not feeling so jaunty as I tried to sound.

We were in a large, gloomy parlor above the bicycle shop. Carlo and Beppo had searched me for weapons and had found none. Forster had dismissed them. I don't know if he carried a gun or not; he didn't look as though he needed one.

I had recognized him immediately from the photograph in our files. The blunt, oversize, somewhat florid features, the easy smile, the frank, feral, widespread eyes, all were there. What I wasn't prepared for was his size. Our description put him down at six feet two inches, 220 pounds. Now I gave him thirty pounds more, and at least another inch.

He was one hell of a big man. According to our records, Forster was supposed to be a physical-culture nut. Also a champion pistol shooter and a fifth Dan black belt. Under the circumstances, I decided not to leap upon him and strangle the life out of him.

"Mr. Nye," he said, "I can't tell you how I have looked forward to this meeting."

"Really?" I answered, quick as a flash.

Forster nodded. "I never really believed that I would one day be sitting with the famous Agent X."

That gave me a nasty turn. My reputation seemed to have spread with astonishing speed. Colonel Baker was getting good service out of his phantom operative; which was fine for him, but not too promising for me.

"Who," I asked, "is agent X?"

Forster shook his head and said, "Sorry, old man. Your cover is blown. You'll just have to face up to it. It must be embarrassing for a man of your reputation, but those are the breaks."

It was more than embarrassing; it looked as if it might be downright fatal. But I decided to concede nothing.

"I don't know what you're talking about," I said.

"Just tell me where I can find Karinovsky."

"I'd be happy to, if I knew anyone by that name."

"Then you refuse?"

"I can't tell you what I don't know."

Forster pursed his lips and thought about that. From his accent, he seemed to be German or Austrian. He was trying to conduct this interview in a light, playful, but distinctly ominous tone; Italy must have affected him that way. Unfortunately, his words came out blunt and heavy. The rapier really wasn't his style; he was better suited for the truncheon. He had a Teutonic sense of humor, which some of us consider distinctly unhumorous. I thought he was ludicrous and extremely dangerous.

"Nye," he said quietly, "haven't you carried it far enough? Surely you know that there are very few secrets of consequence in this world of ours. Ford usually knows what General Motors is doing, and Macy's next move is no mystery to Gimbels. The situation is exactly the same in the various international secret services. After all, our profession does have some traditions. They are unwritten and implicit, but they are traditions all the same."

I listened with interest. All this was news to me.

"Spies spy on each other," Forster continued, "far more than they spy on governments or military installations. And when an agent is captured by the opposing side and identified beyond reasonable doubt, he is supposed to be a good sport about it, tell what he must tell, and leave the posture of grimlipped silence to the professional patriots. Live and let live; history is long, but life is short. It is our tradition. It makes sense, doesn't it, Mr. Nye?"

"Perfect sense," I said.

Forster smiled his most winning smile. "I can understand your feelings. Your reputation is formidable; you wish to preserve it. But I hope that you do not suffer from *hubris*. All of us are human, all of us fail from time to time; even a man of your accomplishments is not immune. And when the time of defeat is upon you, it surely behooves you to deal with it reasonably, to preserve your life in order to fight another day. Don't you think so, Mr. Nye?"

It was the best sermon I had heard in years. He'd practically brought tears to my eyes.

"I agree with you fully," I said.

"Then you will tell me where to find Karinovsky?"

"I don't know where he is."

"But you admit that you are Agent X?"

"Sure. I'll admit to being Agent X, Y or Z, just to please you. But I still don't know where Karinovsky is."

"I am sorry, you must know," Forster said. "After all, this is your operation."

"No, it's not," I said. A bad slip. But he already knew about Guesci.

"Guesci cannot possibly be in charge," Forster said. "The man is an obvious incompetent."

Now was a nice time to find out.

"Guesci can be discounted," Forster continued. "You are in charge and you possess the relevant information."

"I don't know where he is," I said, for at least the fifteenth time.

Forster studied me for a few moments. Then he said, "Mr. Nye, I appeal to your sense of sportsmanship. I beg you not to force me to use —coercion."

He was being sincere. My heart went out to him. I really wanted to spare him the pain of causing me pain.

"I wish I could help you," I said, "but I can't. Will you take my word on that?"

Forster studied me for a few moments. At last

he said, "Yes, Mr. Nye. I will take your word. You may leave."

I stood up, feeling very confused. "You mean I can just go?"

Forster nodded. "I have accepted your word. It is possible that, at the moment, you do not know where Karinovsky is. But you will have to find out. And when you do, we will have another talk."

"As easy as that?" I asked.

"Yes. As long as you stay around Venice, I can find you any time I want. I can do what I please with you. Venice is my base, Nye, not yours. Remember that."

"I'll try to bear it in mind."

I stood up and walked to the door. Behind me, Forster said, "I wonder, Nye, if you are as good as your dossier indicates. In all frankness, you don't look particularly dangerous. A casual observer would judge you barely competent. And yet, your record in the Far East speaks for itself. Specialist in guerrilla warfare. Expert in small arms and explosives. Skilled saboteur and arsonist. Licensed to fly fighter aircraft. A former hydroplane operator and master diver. . . . Have I left anything out?"

"You forgot my medals in lacrosse and jai alai," I said. Inwardly I was cursing Colonel Baker's overreaching imagination. He had poured too much gilt on the lily; in striving to create a paragon, he had only succeeded in producing a paradox.

"It is a fantastic record," Forster said, "but inevitably, a bit difficult to believe."

"Sometimes I find it hard to believe myself," I

told him. I opened the door.

"I would really like to find out how formidable you are," Forster said.

"Maybe some day you will."

"I am looking forward to that day," Forster said. "Goodbye, Mr. Nye."

I left the house and walked through the courtyard. The old man was still polishing his taxi. He nodded at me pleasantly as I walked past him. My back felt itchy. I kept on walking. No one shot me, and I suddenly found myself on the street.

I was safe and sound. It suddenly seemed to me a very good idea to catch the first plane back to Paris. Secret-service work didn't seem to be my line after all. I was thinking about this so hard that I didn't even notice the motorcycle until it pulled up to the curb beside me.

It was a big, high-powered Indian, and the man getting off it was clad in black leather. He was the same man who had ridden beside my taxi.

6

Most of his face was still hidden by immense fur-lined goggles. He had a thin black moustache and a thick lower lip. Sitting on the cycle, he had seemed enormous. Standing on the ground, he was about five feet six, barrel-chested and barrel-bellied.

"Have you a match?" he asked me.

"No," I said. "Will a lighter do?"

"Is it a Flaminaire?"

"Sorry, it's a Silver-Jet."

He nodded approvingly. "I am happy to meet you, Mr. Nye."

"Same here, Mr. Guesci." All that business about matches and lighters was our primary recognition code. As you can see, it was designed so that anyone overhearing us would believe we were carrying on a normal conversation. The secret service is full of clever tricks like that.

"We can't talk here," Guesci said. "We will meet in Venice, in an hour."

I considered telling him that I was going straight back to Marco Polo Airport, and thence to Paris. But frankly, I was ashamed. (Man is the only animal whose fear of embarrassment can overcome his instinct for self-preservation.) And after all, nothing had actually *happened* to me. I decided to wait and see what plans Guesci had. I could cut and run any time I wanted to.

"Where in Venice?" I asked.

"I will tell you," Guesci said. "You will cross this street and take the number six bus, *not* a taxi, and go with it over the causeway to the Piazzale Roma in Venice. Leaving the bus, you will proceed on foot to the Fondamenta della Croce, where you will take a number 1, 2, 4 or 6 vaporetto, but *not* a gondola, to the stop San Silvestro, which is the first stop on your right after passing the Rialto Bridge. Do you know Venice at all?"

"Yes."

Guesci looked doubtful, but continued. "You will find yourself on the Fondamenta dei Vino. Walk back toward the Rialto Bridge, and at the intersection of the Fondamenta with the Calle dei Paradiso you will find the Cafe Paradiso. You will take a table in the sidewalk portion of this cafe and wait for me. Is that clear, or shall I repeat it?"

"Never mind, I'll find the cafe."

Guesci nodded, muttered, "Good luck," and roared away on his motorcycle. I proceeded less spectacularly to the bus stop. Soon I was on the causeway, and Venice was rising from the waves ahead of me.

I didn't know what to think about Guesci, and

this bothered me. It was very important for me to know what kind of a man he was. My life might very well depend on him.

My first impression was not unfavorable. Guesci seemed to be a precise, cautious, humorless fellow, and a careful, even fussy planner. All in all a competent man, though dull.

As it turned out, I could hardly have been more wrong.

7

I left the gray industrial city of Mestre a troubled man; a gray and industrial man, haunted by taxis, stalked by houses, trapped in trolley tracks. My color was soot, my emblem was the traffic light, my theme song was "Arrivederci, Roma," hummed obsessively. But that was before I entered Venice.

My hair became glossier as soon as the bus turned onto the Ponte della Libertà. A chronic acne was entirely cleared up by the time I had crossed the Canale Santa Chiara. When I stood at last in the Piazzale Roma, my metamorphosis was almost complete; but I was still within view of the Autorimessa, with its gasoline stench and its rows of carnivorous Volkswagen beetles. I walked away hastily, covering my trail with cobblestone alleys. I came to the Campazzo Tre Ponti, where five irrational bridges zigzagged across three obsolete canals. There my scales sloughed off and my skin began to breathe.

That is what love can do.

No one would question me if I announced a great and mystic passion for Tahiti or Tibet. But Venice? Did you say *Venice?* Disneyland on the Adriatic? My dear fellow, how can you stand the frantic salesmanship, the indifferent food and insulting prices, the press of the tourist mob; and above all, how can you stand the insufferable *quaintness* of the place?

Friends, I can stand it all easily. In fact, I insist upon it. One does not fall in love by exercise of reason and good taste; one simply falls, and invents ingenious reasons afterwards. One falls in love with one's fatality, whether it be a woman or a city. And all fatalities can be traced to their casual beginnings in childhood.

I had dreamed of canals as a child, nurtured in the green hills of New Jersey, far from Lake Hopatcong, farther still from the sea. In those days I was perhaps the most outstanding twelve-year-old civil engineer east of the Rockies. My first project was the beautification of my home town. My approach was simple and audacious: I flooded the damned place to a mean depth of ten feet.

This eradicated the railroad station, Cooper's Shoestore, a Shell station, a Greek delicatessen, and several other prominent eyesores. The First Presbyterian Church, which lay in a slight declivity, vanished except for its spire. The junior high school was lost with all hands.

After the deluge, we survivors lived quite happily in our submerged town. Many houses were still usable; you could paddle out of your sunken living room and into the watery street. Raising sail, you could proceed between straight rows of trees, their gaunt trunks vanished, looking like enormous flowers. . . .

Years later, when I came to Venice, I saw my youthful dreams realized and transcended. The city was full of details that I had never imagined. Those endless stone lions, for example, were a notable improvement over our two Civil War cannons. I liked the great sagging palazzos more than our neo-Colonial houses; and those striped and slanting barber poles to which gondolas are moored were a huge improvement over our rows of parking meters. Furthermore, I realized in Venice that I had never really explored the enchanting possibilities of boats: fireengine boats and milk barges, ambulance boats with sirens, garbage boats and vegetable boats, and black and gold funeral barges with mournful bearded angels standing in their sterns. . . .

There was my fatality: a childhood dream of a watery transformation. And now, walking through the Salizzada di San Panteleone, I was elated. The canals of Venice surrounded me, the people of Venice jostled me, the churches of Venice watched over me. It seemed to me that Forster belonged to the ugly gray anonymity of Mestre; but Venice was surely mine.

Therefore I ignored Guesci's instructions and made my own way to the Cafe Paradiso. I took a table, ordered a glass of wine, and gradually began to sober up. My spurious childhood dribbled away through the gray flagstones. By the time Guesci arrived, I had returned fully to the present.

* * *

Guesci ordered a Lachryma Christi, drank my health, and asked, "What in God's name happened at the airport? Why did you let those men deceive you?"

I didn't like his tone or his presumption; a man of my reputation should not be condemned so readily. "What makes you think," I asked coldly, "that I was deceived?"

"What do you mean?" Guesci asked.

I had no idea what I meant; but I was in danger of losing Guesci's confidence, which could endanger the entire operation.

"I mean," I said, "that I knew who they were. It was obvious enough."

"Then why did you let them capture you?"

"Because I wanted them to," I said, my lips quirking into a subtle smile.

"But *why?*"

Why indeed? I sipped my wine, and said; "I decided to make a personal estimate of Forster. The best way to do that was to go and see him."

"How absurd!" Guesci cried. "What made you think he would release you?"

"It was in his best interests to let me go."

"What if Forster hadn't agreed?"

"In that case," I murmured, "I would have been obliged—" Here I paused and lighted a cigarette, then looked up and smiled without mirth, "—yes, obliged to convince him, by one means or another."

It sounded almost plausible to me. I waited to see if Guesci would buy it. With a creased and thoughtful face, he did. He said, with a certain grudging respect, "The tales about you, Mr. Nye, are evidently true. Personally, I would not care to be in a room alone with Forster."

"The man cuts a good figure," I conceded, "even if it is somewhat overinflated."

Guesci looked at me with a mixture of irritation and admiration. Then he grinned, shrugged with huge and comic resignation, and patted me on the shoulder. I think he suspected that I was lying; but it was the sort of large-scale, flamboyant lie that appealed to him. As he told me later, only pettiness annoyed him. He delighted in color and movement, and in the protean appearance of things. In this respect, he told me, he was a true Venetian. Like many other subjects of the Serenissima, he believed in style over content, art over life, appearance over reality, and form over substance. He believed simultaneously in fate and free will. He viewed life as a sort of Renaissance melodrama, complete with unexpected appearances and disappearances, heartrending confrontations, preposterous coincidences, disguises and doubles, switched twins and mysteries of birth; all revolving around an obscure and melancholy point of honor. And, of course, he was perfectly right.

Guesci had booked a room for me in the Excelsior, and we went there after finishing our drinks. Through the muslin curtains I could see the elusive reflection of dragons in the Grand Canal. Guesci lay back on a chaise longue, looking terribly old and wise, with his eyes half-closed like a temple cat, smoking a cigarette in the Bulgarian manner. He had shed his businesslike exterior, leaving it perhaps in the saddlebag of his motorcycle. What remained was a pleasant, high-flown fellow direct from the cinquecento.

I asked him how I was supposed to get Karinovsky out of Venice. The answer inevitably involved Guesci in a flight of discursive philosophy.

"To escape from Venice," he told me, "is a profound and disturbing problem. In a very real sense, you could say that no one escapes from Venice, since our city is a simulacre—or worse, a simulaçrum—of the world."

"In that case, let's just escape from Forster," I suggested.

"I'm afraid that doesn't help us," Guesci pointed out sadly. "If Venice is the world, then Forster is that ancient antagonist whom we call Death. No, my friend, in absolute terms an escape of any kind is clearly impossible."

"Why not settle for relative terms?" I asked.

"I suppose we will be forced to. But still, we encounter difficulties. The nature of the city operates against us. Venice owes its very existence to the art of illusion—which is one of the Black Arts. It is a city of mirrors; the canals reflect the buildings, the windows reflect the canals. Distances slide and twist, earth and water interpenetrate. Venice advertises its falsehoods and conceals its truths. In a city like this, events cannot be predicted as in Genoa or Milan. The relative and conditional are apt to turn into the absolute and irrevocable without notice."

"That's really terribly interesting," I said. "But couldn't you attempt a tentative and conditional prediction as to how—relatively, of course—we are going to get out of here?"

Guesci sighed. "Eternally the man of action! My dear Agent X, you have yet to learn the folly of vanity. But I suppose you are anxious to use your much-advertised talents."

I shook my head. "I just want to get Karinovsky out of here in the simplest, safest way."

"Your terms are mutually contradictory," Guesci said. "In Venice, that which is simple is rarely safe; and that which is safe is much too complicated even to consider. However, I have certain hopes. An opportunity presents itself for tomorrow night. It is both simple *and* safe. Relatively."

"Tell me about it."

"A few days ago, a cousin of mine died. He will be buried tomorrow at the Cimitero Communale on San Michele."

I nodded. San Michele is a small rectangular island off the north side of Venice.

"There will be a fine procession for him," Guesci said. "I have hired the very best. My cousin was a Rossi, and his family's name is inscribed in the Golden Book. He died while studying in Rome, but he will be buried as a Venetian."

"That's nice," I said. "But what do you plan to do with Karinovsky and me?"

"I am going to transport you by funeral barge to the Cimitero; then I will load you onto a fishing boat bound for Seno di Tessera. Once on the mainland, the arrangements become easier."

"I suppose you'll transport us there in the casket?"

"So I planned," Guesci said.

"Won't that be rather crowded for your cousin?"

"Not at all," Guesci said. "My cousin is in Rome, still very much alive and studying hard for his examinations. I took the family liberty of borrowing his death."

"Admirable," I said.

Guesci waved away the compliment. "It is an obvious little scheme," he said, "but I think it just might suffice. Assuming, of course, that we get a chance to use it."

"Why wouldn't we?"

"Because it is much *too* simple and clear-cut," Guesci said. "Plans like that would be a certainty in Torino; but they dissolve into nothingness in Venice."

"I think we should give it a try."

"We most certainly will," Guesci said. He sat up and took on a businesslike air. "It is settled. Tomorrow you will meet Karinovsky and proceed with him to the Quartiere Grimani. There, in front of the Casino degli Spiriti, a gondola will await you, and will transport you to the funeral barge in the Sacca della Misericordia. Later I will explain how you find the Casino. Are you armed?"

Colonel Baker had not brought up the question of guns, perhaps fearing that I would do more harm to myself than to an enemy. But I couldn't say this to Guesci. Instead I shook my head, smiled faintly and glanced down at my hands—the merciless hands of Agent X.

"I didn't think you would be," Guesci said. "It would have been foolish of you to carry a weapon through Customs. Therefore I took the liberty of providing for you."

He reached into his breast pocket and took out a huge, sinister-looking automatic. He patted it tenderly on the snout and handed it to me. Somewhat gingerly, I accepted it. Engraving along the barrel told me that it was a French .22 calibre Mab, known as "Le Chasseur."

"Your dossier mentions your preference for a light target pistol," Guesci said. "This was the best I could do on such short notice. It has the 7½-inch barrel to which you are accustomed, but I was unable to find your favorite hollow-point ammunition."

"It doesn't matter," I said. Colonel Baker had really taken pains with Agent X. I wondered what my favorite brand of whiskey was, and whether I favored blondes or brunettes.

"Personally, I would be useless with such a weapon," Guesci said, with a self-deprecatory chuckle. "I use this." He slipped another gun out of his waistband. It was a compact, snub-nosed, hammerless revolver.

"This has the stopping power which an indifferent marksman like myself requires," Guesci said. "Of course, its accuracy is no greater than one would expect from a two-inch barrel."

I nodded and tried to put the massive .22 into my jacket pocket. It wouldn't fit. Finally I slid it under my belt and hoped it wouldn't go off and shoot me in the leg. If it came to gunplay, I was going to be in trouble.

"Where do I meet Karinovsky?" I asked.

"In the building in the rear of the Palazzo Ducale. Karinovsky will meet you at five in the lower galleries, just past the dungeons and near the old charnel house."

I didn't bother to point out that we could have

met just as easily on the Wide Stairs, or in the Ca' d'Oro. Such a meeting place would have been an insult to Guesci's mordant genius. Those who intend to play leading roles in a funeral should very properly meet in a boneyard.

8

The next day, late in the afternoon, I left the Excelsior and proceeded to the Piazza San Marco. I duly admired that grotesque square, renewed my acquaintance with the pigeons, and went on to the Palazzo Ducale. I was not burdened by the huge automatic. Before leaving the hotel, I had told Guesci that the rear sight was badly misaligned. He took my word for it without hesitation, and now his handy little revolver rested in my jacket pocket.

Within the Palazzo I joined a small party of tourists from Göteborg. They were all of a piece; heavy, slow men with cameras, their wives in flowering print dresses and sturdy shoes, with washed-out amiable faces devoid of makeup. They looked at the exhibits weightily, as if to make sure they received full esthetic value. No one would cheat these people of the spiritual goods they had paid for. Beside them, I felt weary, cynical and effete, as though these barbarians were crassly invading my ancient and defenseless homeland. I recognized this as one of the illusions that Venice casts over the visitor.

This cunning city fostered an endless capacity for self-deception. Labyrinthine, it encouraged convoluted thinking. It was the spell of Venice that lured Guesci into expanding the maximum of guile for the minimum of effect. This would have been fatal if Forster had not shared the same weakness. Like Guesci, he mistook complication for profundity. Eternally romantic, he sought dubious modern equivalents for cloak, half-mask and stiletto, and chose a painted-backdrop city upon which to stage the gaiety and terror of his Carnival.

Our guide led us through narrow arched passageways, across shuttered hallways and down winding stone staircases. We passed through endless high galleries. The walls were crowded with pictures, and the guide explained them all.

The mellow afternoon light began to fail; we marched on aching feet into the past of Venice. At one point I smelled orange peels and stagnant water, and knew that the Rio di Canonica di Palazzo was flowing beneath us, and that we were crossing into the old prison. We went down rough-hewn flagstones, and the air was filled with the odor of mold and decaying mortar. My fellow tourists sniffed it with grave pleasure; it was an authentic Renaissance stench. The guide talked about Casanova and the Council of Ten.

We came to the dungeons, and peered into them through tiny barred windows. They were illumined by naked light bulbs and we could see heavy chains stapled into the brick walls. The ossuary was at the end of the corridor, but there was still no sign of Karinovsky. I was getting nervous.

We passed the boneyard and came to the entrance of the Torture Chamber of the Doges, a big new attraction uncovered only last year. We reached it down a narrow winding staircase and past two iron-studded doors. It was a low-ceilinged, oppressive little room, lighted with a single electric bulb. Inside, I recognized the rack and the garrote. In a corner stood the Iron Maiden, her eyes downcast. Various king-sized finger-crushers and pincers hung along the stone walls, and there was a fine collection of chains.

Our guide explained some of the finer points of Renaissance torture. He was reaching some sort of a high point in his dissertation when the light went out.

We were plunged into a thick and incontinent darkness. The ladies screamed and the gentlemen swore, and the guide asked everyone to remain calm and accompany him back to the corridor. I started to move forward with the others, and felt a thick arm slide around my throat. At the same time, something bit into my side at about the location of the kidneys.

"Remain silent," my mugger said. "Do not struggle."

At moments like this, the all-purpose secret agent is supposed to flip his assailant over his shoulder, or kick him where it counts, or make some other positive move that catches the aggressor off-balance and disables him before he can drive in his knife. That is the theory. But I didn't quite see how to bring it off. I was off-balance, gasping for breath, and I had half an inch of knife in my side. Under the circumstances, I decided to bide my time.

The tourists trooped away. They were laughing now, and accusing the guide of staging the whole thing. I heard the first door slam shut; then, more faintly, the second. No one was left in the torture chamber but us chickens.

It grew extremely quiet. Some minutes passed. Then the door creaked open and heavy footsteps crossed the room.

"You may turn him loose."

At that moment, the light came on. Beppo unwound his arm and withdrew his knife from my side. In front of me stood my old buddy Forster.

"Mr. Nye," he said, "I had predicted that we would meet again very soon; but of course, I had no idea that it would be so *very* soon, and in such a convenient place."

I had no snappy comeback for that, so I kept quiet. Forster said, "The Palazzo is closed after five; the last group of tourists is leaving now. With the doors shut, no sound can be heard in the corridor. The guide and the night watchman have received their payment. Mr. Nye, we have a long, undisturbed night ahead of us."

"Forster, you are fiendishly clever," I said. "I am willing to admit that now."

"That is good of you. Will you spare yourself some unpleasantness and tell me where to find Karinovsky?"

"I'd like to know where he is myself," I said. "He was supposed to meet me here."

"But he did not come. Where was your secondary meeting place?"

"We didn't have one."

"Where is Karinovsky living?"

"I don't know."

Forster shook his large and impressive head. "It won't do, Mr. Nye, it simply will not do. You have had ample time to find out where Karinovsky is. If he didn't meet you here, then you must have arranged for another place. Tell me."

I shook my head unhappily.

"I don't like this, Nye; but you force me to use coercion."

I started to tell him again that I knew nothing. He cut me short.

"You know, and you will tell," Forster said. "Since you refuse to be a good sport about it, you can continue the discussion with my colleague, Dr. Jansen."

Forster turned away. I tried to think of something to say. Then I sensed movement behind me, and I remembered Beppo. I started to turn, but something hit me across the back of the head, and I lost consciousness.

9

I awoke to find myself playing a fairly important role in a vintage horror film. My wrists were manacled in front of me, and secured around my waist by a length of chain. This in turn was padlocked to a massive iron staple in the wall. Standing up, I found that I could shuffle a few feet from the floor before the chain brought me up short.

I twisted to one side and felt my right-hand jacket pocket. Guesci's revolver was no longer there. I hadn't thought it would be, but I was disappointed anyhow.

I examined the handcuffs. They were modern and efficient. My chain was heavy enough to moor a tugboat with. The padlock was new, and the staple was firmly set in the wall.

"Are you satisfied with the preparations?" a voice asked. It was a deep, ominous voice, slightly fruity. Enter the mad professer.

I looked around, and for a moment I saw no

one. At last I looked down.

"I am Dr. Jansen," he said.

He was a dwarf, about two and a half feet high, with a large, finely shaped head and blue pop eyes behind heavy glasses. He wore a dark business suit with a rubber apron over it. He also wore a beard. He looked like a tiny Paul Muni playing a miniature Pasteur.

Another man was sitting against the wall, his face almost lost in the shadows. At first I thought it was Forster, come to watch the fun. But it was only Beppo.

"I have monitored your conversations with Mr. Forster," Jansen told me. "My impression was of an intelligent man. I certainly hope so. You see, the effectiveness of coercion techniques—that is to say, their net efficiency in terms of time and energy expended—increases with the intelligence of the subject."

I had never known that. I made no comment on it now. Dr. Jansen, however, seemed used to one-sided conversations.

"Intelligence is, of course, only one factor. Equally important is the patient's degree of susceptibility. This, in turn, is a function of the imagination. I wonder if you know why these two qualities are of such prime importance?"

"No, sir, I don't know why," I said.

"Because one is not—simply—tortured. One also tortures oneself." Dr. Jansen smiled, revealing tiny, even white teeth. I promised myself that some day I would practice painful dentistry on him.

"Without this phenomenon," Jansen said, "a true science of coercion would be impossible.

Brute pain, mindless resistance, and senseless release—that would be the cycle without intelligence and suggestibility."

I told myself that it was a bluff; nobody was going to torture me, nothing was going to happen. But I couldn't make myself believe it. The grinning dwarf with the chubby white hands was getting through to me.

"Perhaps," Jansen continued, "you wonder why I tell you all this?" He smiled subtly and stroked his beard. "It is in order to stimulate the feedback of suggestibility. You must know what to expect, you must brood on it. Your intelligence and your imagination must unleash the supreme torturer within your mind."

I nodded, not paying much attention to him. I was trying to figure out a way of getting out of here with a whole skin. I would even settle for a partial skin. Suppose I gave Forster an address for Karinovsky, any address? That would buy me some time, but not very much. And it might make things tougher.

"My method," Dr. Jansen was saying, "is based upon openness. I explain my theories, and I try to answer your questions. But of course, I can never answer them to your satisfaction."

"Why not?"

"Because all of your questions can ultimately be reduced to one final and unanswerable problem. What you really want, Mr. Nye, is the solution to the old metaphysical problem: Why is there pain? And since I cannot answer that, the very question—following the laws of feedback—tends to potentiate anxiety and augment agony."

He was watching my face carefully while he spoke, probably observing my reactions. (Pupil distention, facial tic, dryness of lips, pronounced digital tremor.)

"Do you have anything to say concerning Mr. Karinovsky?" he asked.

"I don't know where he is."

"Very well," Jansen said. "We will begin." Without haste, he took a pair of rubber gloves from his pocket and drew them on. He turned and looked thoughtfully at the instruments hanging from the wall, finally selecting a pair of pincers about five feet long. They were black, rusted and angular, massively and clumsily jointed. They looked like something you'd use to dejoint an ox. Jansen took the handles in both hands and opened and closed them experimentally. They creaked a little, but the jaws closed with a heavy snap.

He advanced slowly toward me with his king-size pliers extended in front of him. I cowered down against the wall, still not quite believing in what was happening. The pincer jaws opened like the ugly square mouth of a snapping turtle. The mouth was gaping wide and moving toward my face, three inches away, then two, and I tried to get away from it by pressing my head through the wall. When that didn't work I tried to shout, but my throat had shut down. I was so frightened I couldn't even faint.

Then I heard the sound of fists on the door. Someone was shouting, "I have him, I have Karinovsky! Beppo, give me a hand!"

Beppo sprang to his feet and hurried to the door. He opened it, took two steps up the staircase and grunted. He turned and came back with a very annoyed expression on his face. It took me a moment to realize that someone had put a knife into his chest, driving it in clear to the black plastic handle.

Through the heavy doors I could hear the faint crackle of gunfire in the corridor. My rescuer was being kept busy.

Beppo tried to pull the knife out. He got it halfway before he collapsed, almost knocking Dr. Jansen over.

Jansen ducked back hurriedly to avoid him. He was still holding the pincers, and he was a little careless. I managed to grab the free end. I yanked, pulling Jansen off balance before he could let go. As soon as he did, I swung hard with the pincers, hitting him across the ankles and knocking him down. I stretched out and grabbed him by the apron. He screamed and tried to pull away. His apron tore, and he began crawling out of my reach.

I reversed the pincers, pulled the handles open and stabbed out. I caught Jansen's left biceps between the big snapping-turtle jaws, and I brought the handles together.

Jansen's breath whistled out of him so fast that he didn't have time to scream. He writhed around the axis of the pincers like a gaffed salmon, his free hand tearing at the immovable iron mouth. I applied a little more pressure. His face started to turn a yellowish gray. His eyes rolled back into their sockets, and his chin was covered with spittle.

"Give me the key!" I shouted at him. "Give me the handcuff key, or I'll squeeze your arm into a goddamn paste."

That was excessively melodramatic, of course; but I was using a psychological approach.

He pulled the key out of his breast pocket and held it out to me. I started to reach for it, then remembered that we were separated by several feet of pincers. I pulled Jansen toward me, then dropped the pincers and took a grip on his throat. "Unlock me," I told him.

He got the handcuffs off, and then unwound the chain from around my waist. I was free. I hit Dr. Jansen behind the ear with a loop of chain, and he went down hard and didn't move.

I stepped over Beppo and went up the staircase to the corridor. It was dark, and I couldn't see anyone. I thought I heard footsteps to my left, so I turned right and began to run.

10

I ran down endless marble corridors, and I could hear my footsteps echo from the plaster ceilings. I passed rows of narrow medieval windows, and each of them was covered with a modern steel shutter. There were a lot of them, and I began to think I was running in circles. I had a stitch in my side and a cramp in my leg, but I kept on going. Then I found an unlocked door and I went through it into fog and salt air, and the slick round touch of cobblestones. I was outside.

I was on an insignificant street that ran alongside a stagnant canal. To my left was the mouth of a dark alley, far ahead to my right was the halo of a street light. I was lost. Although I couldn't be more than a few blocks from San Marco and the Riva degli Schiavoni, I didn't know in which direction they lay. I turned right and began to pursue the street light.

Venice is an extremely small city unless you want to get somewhere in a hurry. Then its dirty tangle of streets, canals and bridges clings to you like an outrageous old beggar. The city takes on insufferable airs. All of those ridiculous piazzas, small as postage stamps, yet each with five or seven threadlike streets radiating from it—and those endless calles, salizzadas, rios, fondamentas, molos—crossing and recrossing each other like courtiers in a minuet, eternally ready with the exquisite and unnecessary gesture. It is a provincial town pretending to be a metropolis; a superfluous and fantastical monument pretending to be real and necessary. . . . Go to Venice and look at the monuments, spend money, make love—those are its proper pursuits. But never try to save your life. The eccentric old city resents your practicality.

I passed over a humpbacked little bridge and found myself in a concrete courtyard. Gaunt houses rose on all sides with their backs turned to me. Through their blank stucco walls I could hear the sound of television. When I stopped walking, I felt someone else stop.

I moved quickly toward an alley between the buildings. Behind me I heard a sound like a heavy cough and then a sharp crack as brick dust rained on me. Someone had fired with a silenced gun and had scored the wall near my head.

I ran, crossed canals and went through more alleys, and came into a wide square dominated by a church. I thought I recognized the bulge-eyed stone monster that adorned its battlements: Santa Maria Formosa. I had gone in the wrong direction, to a section I didn't know. Behind me was a whisper of footsteps.

I went past the church and into another knot of alleys. The stitch in my side was gone, dissolved by terror. I ran like a grass-fed stallion, and the sound of pursuing footsteps slowly diminished behind me. Agent X had done it again.

But I had congratulated myself a little too early. I cantered to the end of the alley, and had to rein short at an unjumpable stone wall. There was another wall to my left. I whinnied in dismay. Venice had sprung one of her little surprises on me.

On the right, ten or twelve feet up, I saw an ornamental iron balcony. I backed away, took a running jump like a Steeplechase winner, caught the bottom edge and pulled myself up to the rail. The balcony creaked heavily. I managed to swing one leg over the rail. In that awkward position I discovered that someone was trying to jab me in the face with a knife.

"Don't do that," I said.

"Get off that balcony!" she said. I caught a glimpse of black hair and a billowing bathrobe; then I was trying to ward off the knife and nearly going over the balcony backwards.

"Get off!" she screamed.

"All right," I said bitterly. "If you're so anxious to see me killed, I'll get off your damned balcony."

She stopped jabbing. "What are you talking about?"

"I'm in trouble," I said. The girl was American, about twenty-five years old, and nice-looking. No knife-fighter, though.

"I don't believe you," she said.

"Of course not," I said. "Maybe you think I do this for my evening exercise?" She ignored my somewhat hysterical attempt at humor and asked, "What kind of trouble are you in?"

"Serious trouble. Some men are chasing me."

"Why?"

"At the moment," I told her, "I'm in no position to explain."

She looked at me thoughtfully. She was not at all bad-looking. In fact, she could be sensational without the knife. At last she seemed to conclude that I was neither a murderer or a rapist, and perhaps not even a cat-burglar. That left many things I could be, but none of them too much for a Forest Hills girl to handle.

"I don't know," she said. "It's really very strange—"

"Make up your goddamned mind," I said. "I can't hang around here all night."

She frowned and stuck out her lower lip. Cute. I turned my head and got ready to jump back to the street. She said, "Oh, hell, come on in."

I climbed over the rail and walked into her apartment through the tall French windows. She followed me, tying her bathrobe more firmly and keeping the knife handy. I walked to the nearest armchair and sat down. After a while she sat down on the couch and curled her legs under her.

From the chair I could watch most of the street. No one was in sight. Perhaps I had shaken my pursuers, or perhaps they were waiting farther up the block. I lighted a cigarette and tried to think. About my future, mostly. Once again I found that I was filled with doubts concerning my aptitude for secret-service work. Somehow, I just wasn't getting the knack of it. It seemed to me that the best thing might be to fold in my hand, check out of the game, get back to Paris. . . .

"Well?" she asked.

"Well what?"

"Aren't you going to explain?"

"I can't," I told her. "I'm not allowed." After I had said this, it struck me that it might well be true. But even if it wasn't, it seemed to impress her, and it spared me a tedious and somewhat embarrassing explanation.

We exchanged vital statistics. Mavis Somers had gone to Hunter; I had gone to NYU. She lived in a walkup on East Sixty-first near Third; I was a West Villager. Both of us had been in Miami in late February of 1961. She had gone to high school in Summit, New Jersey; I was from nearby South Orange.

We talked, Mavis prepared instant coffee, and we talked some more; we exchanged many inconsequential items, out of which we constructed an invisible network of accord. I did not sweep her into my arms and feel the momentary resistance melt as her arms tightened around my neck and her proud stiff breasts pressed against my white shirt. Shucks, I didn't even think of it. Besides, it would probably happen next time, or maybe the time after. (American men may try to sleep at once with those they like; but they tend to desist for a while with those whom they might love.)

And so the night passed, the dawn birds sang in the charcoal-gray shadows, and morning light crept over the housetops. No sinister figures lurked in the sun-cleansed alleys. I borrowed Mavis' telephone and tried Guesci's apartment. I was surprised when he answered.

Guesci had learned that his plan was compromised half an hour after I left, and he had gone to the Palażzo Ducale to call off the operation. He had found Karinovsky in time; but by then, I was in the torture chamber.

He and Karinovsky had made their rescue raid in commando fashion. Guesci had killed Beppo while Karinovsky guarded the corridor. They had been forced to leave me to take care of Jansen while they fought their way out of the Palazzo. The result: a thigh wound for Guesci; a knife wound in the arm for Karinovsky.

"It was all very unfortunate," Guesci said. "Especially for Karinovsky. There is an irreversible dynamism at work in these matters; a matter of tempo. The efficiency of the hunter increases in proportion to the decline of the hunted. We must get Karinovsky out of here tonight."

I didn't subscribe to Guesci's theory. I knew that Venice was simply too small for this cat-and-mouse game and that Forster had too many men out against us. But even beyond this handicap, I didn't like the way we were rushing into bad moves. Haste makes waste. The way we were going, a hole in the shoulder today might be parleyed into a hole in the head tomorrow.

"Perhaps we should sit tight for a day or two," I said.

"Absolutely impossible," Guesci said. "Aside from everything else, this is the last night of the spring high tide."

That sounded as if it should mean something. It didn't to me. "So what?" I said.

"So we must get Karinovsky out tonight, since my plan depends on the tide."

"That much I understood. But *why* does it depend on the tide?"

"There is no time to explain now," Guesci said. "Karinovsky will give you the necessary details. You will meet him at number 32, Viale di Santazzaro, near the Piazetta dei Leoncini. Do you know where that is?"

"I can find it. But I want to know—"

"There is no time. You must be there at eight-thirty tonight. No sooner or later."

"What if I'm followed?"

"The plan takes that possibility into account," Guesci said.

"I'm very glad to hear it," I told him. "What does the plan suggest that I do about it?"

"You must be very careful, of course. I can't overstress that. Forster's reputation is at stake in this; perhaps even his personal safety, considering the nature of his employers. I strongly recommend that you avoid lonely places. Forster may not be desperate enough to assassinate you in public, although we cannot discount the possibility. Beyond that, I think that the choice of specific courses of action might be most profitably left to your personal judgment."

"Thanks, coach. And where'll you be while I'm choosing my specific courses of action?"

"Waiting for you on the mainland, near Mazzorbo. Karinovsky knows the place. I had planned to accompany you on the escape route, but my leg would only be a hindrance."

I felt ashamed of myself for asking. Hurriedly I said, "How bad is Karinovsky's arm?"

"Bad enough. It gives him considerable pain. But he has a truly fine stamina and determination. Also he has great faith in you, Mr. Nye. I hope you can bring him through."

"I hope so, too," I muttered.

"Now I had better arrange for my own departure," Guesci said. "Good luck!"

He hung up. I did the same, and realized I had forgotten to resign. Typical of me, Anyhow, I couldn't run out with the boys in their present shot-up state. That kind of cowardice takes more courage than I possess.

Mavis said, "My God, you really *are* in trouble."

I nodded morosely.

"Can't you get out of it?"

"It'll be all over in another day," I assured her. And so it would, one way or the other.

We arranged to meet in Paris in a week. She kissed me and told me that I was an imbecile and made me promise to take care of myself. Then I kissed her, and so forth, and Agent X came near to retiring from the Organization, effective immediately. But Mavis spotted a man lounging not far from the building, and I recognized Carlo's sharp features. It was time for Pepe Le Moko to flee once more over the rooftops of the Casbah.

11

I left by a convenient back alley, eluding Carlo without difficulty. It was late morning, and I had considerable time to kill. I took a gondola to the Rialto Bridge and had coffee near the telegraph office. Then I walked around for a while, and then bought a ticket for the afternoon performance at the Teatro Fenice. I slumbered through *Aïda,* left at four-thirty and went for a drink. By five o'clock all was still well. I began to experience a considerable uplift of spirits. This gave me an appetite for the first time in two days, so I went to Leonardi's and gorged on pasta and soup and shrimps Veneta. I paid my bill at six-fifteen and started to leave.

Someone was smiling at me from a table near the door. I smiled back automatically, and then saw that it was none other than Forster. He had just finished his dinner, too. I began to experience a considerable downpress of spirits.

"Mr. Nye," he said, "may I speak with you for a moment?"

"What do you want?" I asked, keeping my distance.

"Really," Forster said, "I won't bite. Do you expect me to machine-gun you here in the restaurant?"

"A silenced pistol would be better," I suggested.

"No, no, not here," Forster said. "Not in Leonardi's." He grinned at me, determined to exercise his whimsy. "This particular place serves the finest scampi in Venice, and therefore has been declared an inviolate sanctuary by all the secret services. Except for the Albanians, of course, who don't count. But an Albanian would never be allowed in here anyhow."

"Nice to hear the local rules," I said, taking a chair.

"We try to keep up appearances. A glass of wine?"

"No, thank you."

"You are cautious about the wrong things," Forster said.

"What did you want to talk to me about?"

"Your departure."

"Am I going somewhere?"

Forster took a long envelope out of his pocket and put it on the table. "Inside this you will find the sum of five thousand American dollars. Also a ticket on Alitalia flight 307 to Paris. Your seat is reserved, and the plane leaves in approximately one hour."

"That's very thoughtful of you," I said, not touching the envelope.

"I enjoy doing favors," Forster said. "It is a

part of my nature. Besides, you will be doing something for me in return. You will tell us where to find Karinovsky, and also save us the trouble of killing you."

"Five thousand isn't much for all that," I said.

"I consider it more than generous. Your departure really isn't worth any more to me."

"Then I think I'll stay, if it's all the same to you."

Forster frowned and said, "No, it is *not* all the same to me. Obviously, it would be convenient if you gave me the information and left. But it would not be a serious hindrance if you didn't. Your influence in this case has become negligible, Mr. Nye."

"Five thousand dollars worth of negligible," I commented.

"Surely you realize that the money is merely a courtesy, a gift to sweeten the taste of defeat. You and I are professionals, we can look at these things honestly. We know that a war consists of many battles; the wise soldier retreats without shame when the odds become too great. We adhere to the logic of the situation rather than the emotion of the moment. Above all, we can face the facts."

"What do you consider the facts?"

Forster took a sip of wine. "Your position has been untenable from the very beginning. We have known all along who you were, whom you worked with, and what your objective was. We have detained you twice in 24 hours, without the slightest difficulty. We know that you are still determined to get Karinovsky out of Venice, and that you will probably make a major attempt tonight. And we know that you haven't got the slightest chance of success."

"Bleak outlook," I said.

"It gets bleaker."

"Go on."

Forster leaned forward earnestly. "Nye, we could have killed you at any time since you came to Venice. The fact that we didn't was solely due to a conflict between Security and Counterespionage. From the viewpoint of Security, you should have been taken out of the game as soon as you were identified. Counterespionage, on the other hand, wanted to let you run as long as possible, in the expectation of following you to Karinovsky. Previously, the requirements of Counterespionage have prevailed."

"And now?"

"Now it is time to close the case. Other matters require our attention; we can't tie up our forces indefinitely while you hurry around Venice. We insist upon knowing where Karinovsky is. We will find him whether you tell us or not. Your refusal to talk now will make matters only slightly more difficult for us, but infinitely more difficult and painful for you. We will get the truth out of you anyhow. But the only reward for stubbornness will be a quick death. What do you say?"

Forster held the envelope out to me, and I felt shaken because he really expected me to take it, and my refusal seemed naive and suicidal. But I stood up and shook my head.

"Very well, Mr. Nye," Forster said. "Since you refuse the pleasant, civilized way, we are forced to use the unpleasant, uncivilized way. We will ask you about Karinovsky again very soon; but next time we will ask with more firmness."

And that was that. I left the restaurant. Outside, the sun was going down.

12

I told myself that I was in a very serious situation. But I found it difficult to believe. There was a warm sunset glow on the old buildings. The canals sparkled a brilliant blue and brown. A thousand people pushed past me along the narrow streets. An unshaven man tried to sell me a toy gondola while real gondolas glided past. There was a smell of roasting coffee in the air. The sunlight, the crowds, the narrow protective streets, the gleaming water, all conspired to lull me into a dangerous sense of security.

I walked for a while, then caught a vaporetto near the Teatro Malibran. It was as crowded as a New York subway at rush hour. I was able to hang on to a pole in the center of the boat.

A squat workman clung to the pole beneath my left arm. Directly facing me, almost embracing me, was an attractive blonde girl in a green sweater, carrying an art portfolio. We bumped and recoiled and stared vacantly over each other's left shoulder.

Pressed close against me on my right was a red-faced tourist in a stiff tweed sports jacket with complicated flaps and buttons. He had a heavy camera slung around his neck and a battered pigskin briefcase cradled in his arms. Beside him, unable to gain a handhold, was a small unshaven man in a black suit, with a faint lipstick smear on the edge of his mouth. Near him was a tall youth with a freckled face and an enlarged Adam's apple. He was trying to maneuver himself into position beside the blonde girl. His progress was blocked by an immovable old lady in a raincoat.

The vaporetto passed the Campo di Mars and swung wide into the Grand Canal. The crowd swayed. The blonde girl's breasts pressed for a moment against my jacket. The lipsticked man nearly lost his balance, and the workman stood like a weathered rock. The youth with the Adam's apple tried to edge around the old lady; he was blocked by her umbrella. The blonde girl edged away from me, and the red-faced tourist shuffled for footing.

I felt a sharp pain in my left side.

Someone whispered, "Where is he?"

It was the tourist; his beefy red face was inches from my shoulder. His briefcase pressed into my side. He said, "Mr. Forster sent me to ask you."

"I don't know what you're talking about," I said. Something stabbed me again in the side. The vaporetto made a turn and the crowd swayed. I was able to glance down and see that my jacket was ripped. Blood was trickling down my trousers.

"Just tell me where he is," the man said. And again something stabbed at me, in the side just below the ribs.

The boat turned sharply again, and this time I noticed the tourist's briefcase. A drop of blood oozed out of a fold along its bottom right-hand corner. I stared at it stupidly. The fold of leather winked at me; a steely little glint of light flashed for a moment from a concealed knife-blade in the spine of the briefcase, then darted out of sight.

"The blade is spring-loaded," the tourist told me. "It's length is adjustable. I am now using approximately one half inch."

"You're out of your mind," I said.

"Tell me where he is," the man said. "Tell me, or I'll carve your side into tournedos."

I looked around. Nobody in that crowd had noticed a thing. The blonde girl was trying to keep her left breast out of my jacket pocket. The old lady was still blocking the youth. The lipsticked man was reading an airform. The workman was stolidly holding his ground. The red-faced man was carving my side into tournedos.

"I'll call for help," I told him.

"Just as you please."

I saw him press the handle of the briefcase, and I pushed myself away from the flickering little blade, colliding with the blonde girl. She staggered back and looked at me with disgust. The move had done no good. The red-faced man had simply moved with me, filling up the space I had vacated.

He moved his briefcase into position again, but a lurch of the boat threw him off-balance. He missed my side and carved a gash across the top of my belt.

"Tell me," he said.

I tried to move away again, but the crowd wouldn't yield. Was I going to stand here and be slashed to death by a red-faced man in a ridiculous jacket? In Venice, in a vaporetta, in the middle of a dense crowd? My side was soggy with blood. The man was pressing against me, sweating with concentration. I could feel his body stiffen as he got ready to strike again with his spring-blade briefcase. The crowd was oblivious to our little drama. They were staring over each other's shoulders, or watching the progress of the Adam's-appled youth, who had finally succeeded in sliding around the old lady's umbrella.

The briefcase moved and I jerked back. He grazed me lightly across the ribs. People glanced at me, then turned their attention back to the youth.

Suddenly I was filled with a murderous and righteous rage. I reached down between the folds of tightly pressed clothing, located the man's belt, positioned my hand and squeezed hard in the vicinity of his testicles.

He screamed. People turned and stared at him. I turned also, frowning in bewilderment. The man was clutching his groin with both hands. "Anything wrong?" I asked him.

During the excitement, the youth finally reached the side of the blonde girl. Now that he had attained his objective, he didn't seem to know what to do.

The red-faced man groaned. He couldn't seem

to get his breath. I said, "It seems to be an attack of some sort."

"Loosen his collar," the old woman said.

I reached out toward his throat. He gasped and swung wildly with his briefcase, stabbing the workman. The workman whirled and struck him at once with a large, shapeless brown fist. During the confusion, I stamped down hard on the red-faced man's right instep.

The youth, seeing his opportunity and regaining his wits, said to the blonde girl: "Some business!" She pretended not to hear him. The workman was trying to apologize to the red-faced man. He, looking sick and shaky, seemed to be out of action for the immediate future.

The vaporetto swung in to a pier. I pushed my way off. I began walking, and I didn't look back.

13

My left leg was beginning to stiffen, and blood was squirting through the eyelets of my shoe. The sun was just down, but an antique golden glow filled the street, casting an air of spurious transformation upon the crowd. Venice was up to its old tricks again, and I was faint-headed enough to enjoy it.

Then I slipped on the slimy cobblestones. My left leg buckled, and I started to fall. A hand gripped me and pulled me to my feet.

The man who had helped me was tall and strongly constructed. His face was at once amiable and cruel. He wore a light-weight gray worsted of exemplary fit. A light blue-gray ascot, the smoky color of his eyes, was knotted carelessly and tucked into a shirt of raw Italian silk. A bulky Rolex Oyster Navigator clung to his wrist; with its black face and luminous hands and dots it resembled a tropical spider.

"Anything the matter?" he asked, in a pleasant British voice.

"Dizzy spell," I said. "Thanks for catching me." I made a tentative movement to free my arm.

"No trouble," the man said. He released my arm; the movement gave me a glimpse of a .32-calibre Beretta with a skeleton grip and depressed sights, and tucked into a plain chamois shoulder holster.

"You seem to have hurt your leg," he said.

"I slipped when I left the vaporetto."

The man nodded, studying the slashes in my pants leg and across my shoe. "One must be careful of Venetian piers," he said. "They cut rather like razors, don't they?"

I shrugged. The stranger smiled. "Here on holiday?" he asked.

"More or less. Right now I'm looking for the house of a friend of mine. But these streets are somewhat confusing."

"Well," he said, "I know this place tolerably well. Perhaps I could direct you."

Alarm bells rang in my head. I ignored them, having heard no other sound for quite some time. I had to assume that I was being followed, and that another assault was being prepared against me. If this self-possessed stranger were one of the enemy, he had already had ample opportunity to make his move. If he were not, his presence might give Forster something to think about, and perhaps even force him to modify his plans. I didn't see where I could lose by keeping him with me.

"I am looking for the Via di San Lazzaro," I told him.

"I believe I know the street," he replied. "Let me think a moment." Three vertical lines of concentration creased his forehead. "Yes, of course. Directly behind the Piazetta dei Leoncini, and terminating in the Molo. One would usually walk through the Piazza San Marco; but there is a shorter route past the Basilica, to the entrance of the Merceria, and then through that alley rather grandiloquently called 'Salizzada d'Arlecchino.' Shall I guide you?"

"I wouldn't want to take up your time."

"Time to burn," the man said, with a short, not unpleasant laugh. "My company sent me down here on a job, but it seems that it's off."

"Your company?"

"Bristol Business Systems." He led me toward the Merceria. "My name is Edmonds, by the way. I travel in business machines. At the last minute, some American firm outbid us for this particular contract."

"That's interesting," I said. "I'm in business machines, too."

Edmonds nodded. "Somehow, I thought that you were."

I stared at him. Business machines, a special contract, and a skeleton-grip Beretta. Could this be my British opposite number? The coincidence would be too great anywhere except in Venice, where the machinery of illusion delights in casting up the improbable, the unusual, and the unexpected. There is a price, of course; by tampering with probabilities, Venice induces a deterioration in the commonplace—to her disadvantage.

Edmond's hard, mocking face betrayed nothing. I said, "I'm sorry to hear that you lost the contract."

"It really doesn't matter," Edmonds said. "There's plenty of work for us all. As it happens, I've been reassigned to Jamaica."

"Is there much demand for business machines there?"

"Enough, for the models I deal in."

"They must be unusual."

"Versatile, I'd call them."

"Then you'll be leaving Venice soon?"

"I fly out in three hours. That gives me just enough time for a flutter at the tables."

I must have looked puzzled. Edmonds explained, "I mean the gambling tables over at the Lido. Baccarat and chemin-de-fer are the main attractions, of course, but I'm anxious to try the roulette. Not everyone knows it, but the house advantage has been lowered this season in an attempt to overtake Monte Carlo. It presents certain opportunities."

"Sounds interesting," I said.

"Care to join me? I'm going out there now."

"I really would like to," I told him, "but I can't."

"I quite understand," Edmonds said. "Well, here we are. The Via di San Lazzaro, in all its fusty magniloquence."

I thanked him, but Edmonds waved a deprecating hand. "Sorry I can't stay around and show you the sights. Perhaps I could help you not to trip on any more piers. But time and tide. . ."

With an airy wave of his hand, Edmonds was

gone, taking with him a spirit of easy competence and reliability. I looked at my watch. It was nearly eight o'clock. I began walking slowly down the street, looking for house numbers.

14

A faint red glow flickered between two black buildings; then it was gone, missing and presumed drowned in the Laguna Morta. The night wind whispered threats to the chimneys. The waters of the canal chewed with a soft toothless mouth on decaying stone piles. The high-shouldered old houses huddled together for comfort. Renaissance figures walked on the sunken street, dressed in twilight blue and pretending they were alive. They didn't fool me; I knew a *danse macabre* when I saw one.

I came to the end of the Via di San Lazzaro where it turned into the Rio Terra Maddalena. I was looking for number 32, but the street ended with number 25. I looked, I searched, I stared. There was no 32. The back of my neck began to tingle.

I retraced my route and tried to think. Unfortunately, my mind wasn't interested in house numbers. It insisted upon showing me an illuminated slide show of a sniper high above the street leaning through a shuttered window, with my head trapped in his telescopic sights.

I forced myself to think of pleasanter things. Of strangling Forster, for example, or disemboweling Colonel Baker. Of miraculously escaping from Venice and living out the rest of my life as a simple sheep herder in South Australia.

Where was that damned address? Had I gotten it right? 32, Via di San Lazzaro. Or could Guesci have said *Calle* di San Lazzaro. Or *Viale. . .*

That had to be it. I asked and got directions. The Viale di San Lazzaro was some distance away, in the Cannareggio ward. I hurried through dusk and charcoal fumes, crossed the Station Bridge, made various left and right turns, and reached the general vicinity. But then I was caught in a snarl of alleys off the Calle della Massena.

There were fewer tourists in this section. Workmen and souvenir-sellers passed me, and an off-duty gondolier. I received cryptic directions from a fat woman with a basket of laundry, and passed a group of noisy children shepherded by a nun. Then a little boy in a white sailor's suit came by, and after him a hip-booted fisherman.

The fisherman moved on. The little boy stopped, danced from one leg to the other, and raised a pea-shooter to his mouth. I heard a dry rattle as the pea hit the wall behind me. The boy grinned, turned, and shot at a stately lady dressed in black with a shopping basket under her arm. The lady reached involuntarily for her backside, stopped herself, and cursed the boy in an unfathomable dialect. The boy jumped up and down, and the old lady continued down the street.

The boy looked around for a new target, took aim at me again and fired. I raised my arm, heard the puff of his breath, and felt something tug at the sleeve. I examined the sleeve and found a tiny dart imbedded in the cloth, its back a piece of cotton wadding, its front an indigo-stained needle.

Then the streetlights came on. In their yellow glare I saw the boy's face, still grinning, his forehead wrinkled under the sailor's cap, his eyes dark and pouched, his nose sharp with deep lines running from the nostrils to the sides of his mouth, his chin and cheeks covered with a powdered stubble. It was none other than my old friend, the malignant dwarf.

I stared. It was Jansen, bereft of his beard, his teeth bared in an evil grin. Jansen masquerading as a pea-shooter. He fired, and I dodged. The dart missed my neck by inches; I wondered if he had tipped it with curare or strychnine, or with some noxious fluid of his own distillation.

Jansen danced and giggled in a poor but sufficient imitation of childish high spirits. Several strollers laughed. Jansen fitted another dart into his gun.

I wanted badly to rush him before he had time to fire, and to drop-kick him into the canal. But a crowd had collected to watch the fun. And at least three people in that crowd were not amused.

One of them was Carlo. One was the red-faced shoefighter from the vaporetto. And the third was the fat man who had taken my taxi when I first arrived at Marco Polo airport.

Then I understood the premise of the scene that Forster, with his taste for dubious tableaux, had arranged for me. Maddened with rage, I was supposed to assault the dwarf before he had time to puncture me with his indigo needles. The crowd, apparently seeing a child thus attacked, would react with violence. During the scuffle, Carlo would slip a knife between my ribs.

I turned and walked away. Forster's men followed, and Jansen skipped along in front of them. I lengthened my stride, wondering about the effective range of his peashooter.

I tried to lose myself in the complex interconnections of streets and canals and bridges. But the streetlights threw my treacherous shadow behind me; I dragged it after me like a tail. I crossed a bridge, went down an alley, and found myself in the Ghetto Vecchio, in front of the little synagogue. As usual, I was lost. I turned a corner and found myself on the Viale di San Lazzaro. I wasn't particularly surprised. In the maze of Venice it is difficult to find anything quickly; but it is equally difficult to lose anything for long.

Number 32 was at the end of the street near the canal. It lay behind a high stone wall with a glitter of broken glass on top. There was a heavy iron gate, which was locked. I shook it, heard the bolt slide, and the gate swung open. A voice said, "Hurry!"

I went through the gate, took a few blind steps in the darkness and something knocked me down. I got up and saw that it was a stone cupid.

The gate closed and the bolt slammed home. Then Karinovsky was standing beside me, gripping me fiercely by the shoulder.

"Nye!" he said. "My dear friend, you are late. I began to fear that you would not come."

"I was unavoidably detained," I heard myself say in a light, amused voice. "But you should have known that I wouldn't miss this for anything."

I had spoken in the voice of vanity: that quality which serves so well in place of courage, and which is almost indistinguishable from it.

15

Behind the stone wall was a barren little garden, and just past that was a house. Karinovsky led me inside, waved me to a chair, and offered me a drink.

"I cannot honestly recommend the slivovitz," he said. "Guesci must have sent it as a joke. But the Lachryma Christi, despite its unconvivial name, is an honest drink."

I took wine and studied the man I had come to rescue. Karinovsky's left arm was carried high on his chest in a black silk sling. Aside from that, he seemed as tough and competent as ever. I had forgotten the faintly Mongol tilt to his eyes, and how his black hair was touched with a distinguished feather of gray. He had that look of amused and ironic detachment which comes to men who live through rapid changes of fortune; South American presidents, for example. I was glad I had come, and hoped I could be of service.

"How is your arm?" I asked.

"Serviceable," he said. "Luckily for me, my attacker was using a mere half inch of point."

"That's enough to cut your throat with."

"Such was his intention, which I foiled by a clever movement of my shield-arm. Unfortunately I was lacking a shield."

"What did you do?"

"I decided that the fellow was entirely too fast for an old fellow like me," Karinovsky said, spreading his hands in a pathetic gesture. "So I slowed him down by the simple expedient of breaking his back."

I nodded, wanting to applaud but restraining myself. I have always been a sucker for the grand manner.

"But you also seem to have had your troubles," Karinovsky said, glancing at my torn left leg.

"A scratch," I assured him. "It was my misfortune to meet a man with extremely sharp shoes."

"One meets all kinds in Venice," Karinovsky said, and settled back comfortably in his chair. All part of the grand manner. But a little irritating, since the success of his pose depended upon my playing the alarmed straight man.

I was damned if I was going to do it. I took out my cigarettes, offered one to Karinovsky, lit one for myself. We blew out gray plumes of contented smoke. I thought I heard footsteps in the garden. Karinovsky offered me another drink. The iron gate rattled suddenly. I decided to play the straight man.

"All right," I said. "What do you suggest we do now?"

"I suggest that you rescue me."

"And how do you suggest that I go about it?"

Karinovsky flicked ash from the end of his cigarette. "Knowing your boundless resources, my friend, and your collection of varied skills, I have no doubt that you can find a way. Unless, of course, you prefer to follow Guesci's somewhat dubious scheme."

"Dubious?"

"Perhaps I don't do it justice," Karinovsky said. "Guesci's plan is certainly very ingenious. Perhaps a little too ingenious, if you know what I mean."

"I don't. I don't even know what his plan is."

"It will amuse you," Karinovsky said. "It is based, of course, upon your renowned and diverse talents."

I felt a sudden cold chill. What had Guesci planned for us? And what did it have to do with the talents of Agent X? I tried to remember what accomplishments were imputed to me, and I couldn't. I felt that it was time to clear up the situation.

"Karinovsky," I said, "about those skills—"

"Yes?" he said pleasantly.

"I'm afraid they may have become exaggerated in the retelling."

"Nonsense," he said.

"No, really. As a matter of fact, I'm quite an untalented person."

Karinovsky laughed. "It is apparent that you are given to sudden attacks of modesty," he said. "It is a chronic disease of the Anglo-Saxon mentality. Next you'll be telling me that you don't really consider yourself a secret agent."

I managed to produce a sickly grin. "That would be going a little too far," I said.

"Of course," he said. "Come now, we'll have no genteel disclaimers. Not between us, my friend."

"All right," I said. Apparently it was not the time to clear up the status of Agent X. "But remember—I may be a trifle rusty."

"Accepted. Some more wine?"

"No, thank you. Let's get down to business. This house is probably surrounded, you know."

"Guesci's plan assumed that eventuality."

"Are we supposed to walk out of here disguised as delivery men?"

"Nothing so obvious."

"Then how?"

"Let us examine the problem," Karinovsky said, with infuriating nonchalance. "What do you think about a flight over the rooftops?"

"Forster must be prepared for that."

"True. But what about the canal? Could we make our escape by boat, do you think?"

I shook my head. "Forster would have thought of that. The canals of Venice are fairly conspicuous."

"Very well," Karinovsky said. "The obvious exits are blocked. Now, following Guesci's line of reasoning, we must look to the inobvious. That is to say, we must seek out the apparently impractical, the unreasonable, the unlikely. We must do what Forster does not expect; or better, we must do what he has never even considered. We must—"

Karinovsky's flight of oratory was ended by the sound of glass breaking upstairs. For a moment there was silence, and then we heard something land on the floor with a heavy thump.

"Commando tactics," Karinovsky said scornfully. He leaned back and lighted another cigarette. I wanted to stuff it down his ham actor's throat.

We could hear the man or men upstairs moving cautiously in the darkness. Then the outer gate began to rattle. There was a brief ringing noise; it sounded as if the bolt had been cut. After a moment, we could hear the gate creak open.

"I suppose," Karinovsky said, "that we should be on our way."

He stood up, slipped his left arm out of the sling, and glanced at his watch. He took a final drag on his cigarette and stamped it out on the carpet. Then, having run out of gestures, he led me out of the room and down a hallway.

We stopped beside a heavy wooden door. A flashlight was set in brackets beside it. Karinovsky took the flashlight and pulled the door open. We entered, and he threw the bolts.

We went down a shallow staircase into a bare stone chamber. The walls were watersoaked, and smelled of sour antiquity: an odor compounded of garlic, mud, crushed granite and stagnant water. There was an iron door in the far wall, and something lay in a shapeless heap beside it.

Karinovsky crossed the room and opened the iron door. I saw a gleam of light upon water. We were at the canal entrance of the house.

I started to lean out, but Karinovsky pulled me back. "You might be spotted," he told me. "I am quite sure that Forster has this exit under surveillance."

"Then how do we reach the boat?"

"We have no boat out there," Karinovsky said. "We crossed out that possibility, did we not?"

I heard footsteps on the floor above us. Then there was a sound of blows on the door to our chamber.

"So what do we do?" I asked. "Swim?"

"After a fashion," Karinovsky said. He pointed his flashlight at the heap near the door. I saw bright yellow cylinders, splay-footed fins, air regulators, and grotesque black rubber masks with oval cyclops' eyes.

"We swim," Karinovsky said, "but in a manner that Forster might not have anticipated. I am sorry for the delay; but we had to wait for full high tide, otherwise some of the canals on our route are impassable. Now I suggest that we change rather hurriedly and make our departure. The door might not hold for long."

16

I didn't know whether to laugh or cry, to give praise for cleverness or curses for folly. Perhaps fortunately, there was no time to evolve an attitude. We changed quickly and adjusted our face masks. Forster's men were hammering at the door, and the hinges were beginning to tear loose. Karinovsky bit down on the mouthpiece of his regulator and slipped into the dark water of the canal. I followed close behind. As I went in, I heard an angry shout. I turned my head and saw a boat less than twenty feet away. Forster had not overlooked the water gate.

I could just make out Karinovsky's flippers ahead of me. The water was warm and faintly slimy, and it smelled of sewage and marsh gas. I controlled a desire to retch, and followed Karinovsky to the bottom of the canal, a depth of perhaps ten feet. He turned left, found the canal wall for a guide, and began to swim strongly. I had to work hard to stay up with him.

I knew roughly where we were. Karinovsky's house had fronted on the wide Rio San Agostin, near the center of the city. He had turned left, following the canal under the Calle Dona and the Calle della Vida bridges. If we continued long enough in this direction, and if we succeeded in finding our way through the intricate canal system, we would come out on Venice's northern periphery, facing the lagoon and the encircling mainland. At the moment, the plan seemed eminently reasonable, though not for tender stomachs.

I stayed less than a foot behind Karinovsky's flippers, gliding just above a bottom of foul-smelling black mud. My fingertips brushed the gummy outlines of a barrel, a half-buried plank, the edge of a steamer trunk. The canals of Venice serve as unofficial garbage dump for the bordering houses. This one evidently had not been drained and cleaned in a long time. We swam through a thin, revolting soup in which orange peels, half-eaten bananas, eggshells, lobster claws and apple cores hung in suspension. It was quite unpleasant. I tried to convince myself that it was preferable to a last desperate run through narrow alleys.

Karinovsky's fingertips located an intersection and swung right into the Rio San Giacomo dall'Orio. As we turned, there was a muffled explosion overhead, and I saw a small, shiny object plunge past me and bury itself in the sand. I looked upward and saw a long, narrow shadow like a monster barracuda glide near me.

I braked, letting it slip past. Karinovsky had done the same. The boat from the water-gate had evidently given chase. From its length and shape, I knew that it was a gondola.

The strong yellow finger of a searchlight probed the water. I could hear men talking. The gondola was braked expertly, and then began to slide backward. Karinovsky tugged at my arm, gestured, and I nodded. We sprinted under the boat's keel, toward the Terra Prima bridge. I knew almost at once that we weren't going to make it.

The silent gondola, propelled by its single big oar, was easily capable of four times our speed. Our position was given away by the telltale stream of bubbles from our respirators. Glancing back, I saw the narrow black shadow of the gondola overhauling us. The searchlight beam rested on my back, and I heard the dull explosion of a gun.

The bullet missed me by inches. Karinovsky was swimming hard, and I gritted my teeth and kicked, trying to shake off that clinging yellow light.

Then I saw what Karinovsky had spotted: a huge rectangular darkness beneath the Terra Prima bridge. We reached it and found a flat-bottomed work barge, moored for the night. There was barely two feet of room for us between its barnacled keel and the glutinous mud bottom.

The gondola swept past, then came to a stop. The searchlight poked and probed, and the gondola inched backward. There was a crisp rasping of wood as they came alongside the barge; a sleepy, outraged voice asked them what in hell they were doing.

At the height of the argument we sneaked out from under the barge and continued up the Rio di San Baldo. We were gaining valuable yards while an argument raged between bargemen and gondolier. Then it was broken off abruptly, and the gondola's oar splashed and gained a purchase on the water. Again, our air bubbles must have given us away.

We were in a wide stretch of the canal, and the gondola was coming up fast. Karinovsky turned hard to his right, continued for a dozen yards, and turned right again, as if to enter the Rio Maceningo. But he straightened out and continued to the Rio della Pergola. The gondola hesitated at the entrance to Maceningo, losing time in tracing the path of our bubbles.

We went by the heavy wooden piles of Santa Maria Mater Domini, and turned left, into a waterway about five feet wide. I thought we must have lost the gondola; but when I looked back, I saw the marching yellow point of its searchlight about thirty feet behind.

It came straight into our narrow waterway, filling it and scraping the embankment on either side, but still gaining on us. A man in the bow was shouting encouragement to the gondolier, and the barracuda shape crept up behind me. I wanted to tell Karinovsky that we were trapped, that we had better make an attempt to turn back under the boat. I tugged at his leg. He turned and grinned, patted the top of his head and swam on.

I couldn't understand what he meant. The searchlight was on us again, and they had begun firing. Then Karinovsky disappeared.

Immediately after that, I disappeared.

I was in complete darkness. Stone scraped my left arm. I straightened out and hit my head against the right wall. I thought I could hear triumphant voices behind me, and I scraped again on the left. The passage couldn't have been more than three feet wide. Then I was out of it, swimming through the lighter gloom of a canal.

We surfaced. The spires of the Mater Domini filled the night sky behind us. We had followed a canal that ran beneath the church. It might have been passable for gondolas at low tide, but at high tide it was completely flooded.

Karinovsky said, "We'll have to keep on going. They can back out and come around by way of the Maceningo Canal in five minutes."

"Where are we going?" I asked.

Karinovsky gestured boldly. "Like Lord Byron, we are going to swim across the Grand Canal. After that our quickest way would be straight up the Canale della Misericordia and into the Lagoon. But we can't risk so obvious a route. For safety's sake we shall do a little extra swimming through the Quartiere Grimani. I will take you by the scenic route, of course."

"Thanks. Will our air tanks hold out?"

"I hope so."

"You don't think we can try it on foot now?"

"No. Forster may have a dozen men on foot, but surely no more than a few in boats. The odds favor us in the water."

I was about to ask what we would do when we reached the Lagoon. But then I noticed the harsh lines of strain on Karinovsky's face.

"How is your arm?"

"Proving more of a nuisance than I had expected. But not enough to impede us, I think. Now we had better—"

Someone shouted at us from the embankment: "Hey, what in hell is going on out there?"

We submerged, moved quickly past San Stae, and into the Grand Canal. Halfway across, Karinovsky came to the surface, lined up the Palazzo Erizzo and the Maddalena Church, and submerged again. It seemed to me that he was swimming more slowly, and at a greater expenditure of energy.

A vaporetto churned past us, and then a work barge. Twenty minutes later we had crossed the seventy-odd yards of the Canal, and were entering the dog-leg Rio della Maddalena.

It seemed safe enough here. We swam undisturbed into the Rio dei Servi, and followed its winding course into the Rio di San Girolamo. After passing the Ghetto Nuovo, Karinovsky led us by a connecting channel into the Rio della Sansa. A gondola passed over us, but no searchlight reached into the water, and no voice shouted an alarm. Instead, a cracked tenor sang a Neapolitan love song, and a girl giggled.

The canal turned right, and we lost contact with the retaining wall. When we surfaced, I saw that we were in the Venetian Lagoon. The city lay just behind us, its glistening spires and tilted domes rising from the water like a romantic sketch of Atlantis. A mile or so ahead of us was the marshy Veneto coast; to our right was the island of Murano, and very close on our left was Venice's causeway to Mestre.

"Do we swim across the Lagoon?" I asked.

"No," Karinovsky said, "We are spared that. We merely follow the shoreline around the Sacca di San Girolamo, to a position near the Ricovero Penitenti. Once there, our troubles should be ended."

He was floating with difficulty, his head thrown back and the breath rasping in his throat. He turned over and began to swim, slowly and doggedly, following the contour of the land to the west. In ten minutes we reached a low, flat, deserted piece of land near the entrance to the Cannareggio Canal, almost opposite the slaughterhouse. The Ricovero was fifty yards away, half-hidden behind its stone walls.

"Behold!" Karinovsky said proudly.

I saw the boat, dark and sleek, moored to the seawall. Something about its long low hull disturbed me, touching a memory just beyond recall. Suddenly I wanted nothing to do with that boat. But my feeling was illogical and absurd, so I ignored it and followed Karinovsky to the boat, which we boarded by means of a ladder.

17

No one was aboard. We got rid of the air cylinders and crept down the narrow deck into the cockpit. We sat for a while and caught our breath, then changed into dry clothes that had been stored for us under the seat. I was very tired from the long swim, and Karinovsky looked close to exhaustion. But we couldn't afford to rest now. We had shaken off our pursuers, at least for the moment; but we had to use our advantage before they had a chance to find us again.

Karinovsky opened the dashboard compartment and took out a map and a small flashlight. The map showed the northern part of the Laguna Veneta, from the Causeway to Torcello.

"This is our position," Karinovsky told me. "The causeway is on our left, San Michele and Murano on our right, the mainland straight ahead to the north. We follow the main channel, marked here in red, past Isola Tessera, to the vicinity of Marco Polo Airport. But we do not go to the airport wharf."

"Of course not," I said. "That would be too easy."

"Too dangerous," Karinovsky amended. "We turn eastward before reaching the wharf, take the channel past San Giacomo in Palude, and continue nearly as far as Mazzorbo. Do you see Mazzorbo circled there?"

"I thought it was a flyspeck. What kind of chart is this?"

"Albanian. It is a copy of a Yugoslav naval chart."

"Couldn't Guesci have gotten us an Italian chart?"

"The Government Printing Office was out of stock. The Lagoon is being resurveyed."

"A British Admiralty chart would have been best of all."

"Guesci couldn't very well write to London for one, could he?"

"I suppose not."

"In any event, he assured me that a child could navigate by this. Look, the main islands and channels are clearly marked. All you have to do is steer for the airport, then turn right at the next-to-last marker and continue toward Mazzorbo, then turn left at number 5 marker and follow the channel into Palude del Monte."

Karinovsky spread his hands to show how easy it would be. I was not so sure. I had done some day-sailing on Long Island Sound, enough to know how tricky it could get trying to follow a nautical chart at night across an unfamiliar body of water.

I examined the chart. Its markings were conventional. Channels were shown in a series of bold dashes. Navigational aids were white or red dots. Marsh or sandy areas were shaded with little blue crosses; there were plenty of them. Depths in the Lagoon reached a low tide maximum of six feet, but the average was more like three. There were entirely too many places to run aground, and to do so now, on a falling tide, could be disastrous.

Karinovsky was beginning to fidget, but I took a moment to examine the boat. She was a flat, unlovely, shark-headed old beast, paint-sick and scarred, with a fin in the rear and a massive ten feet of engine cowling in the bow. That cowling looked big enough to house a truck engine. The dashboard had the usual array of controls; nothing very much out of the ordinary except for something called a "trim-tab." I didn't know what it was, so I decided to leave it alone. There were two tachometers, one for the engine and one for the supercharger. There was a bronze plaque in the center that gave the boat's vital statistics: 28 feet 6 inches long, 11 feet 6 inches wide, gross weight of 5,200 lbs. Engine: Rolls Royce Merlin. Horsepower: 2,000.

Horsepower two thousand? I stopped and reread the plaque. Yes, Virginia, there is a horsepower two thousand. All of that horsepower is contained within your lively Rolls Royce Merlin engine. It is the very same engine, you may remember, that was used during World War II to power the Mosquito fighter-bomber. . . .

"What homicidal maniac," I asked, keeping my voice low and level, "procured this bomb for us?"

"You are speaking about the boat? Guesci found it, of course."

"Then let Guesci drive it."

"A boat is a boat," Karinovsky said sharply.

"The hell it is," I told him. "This is no boat. This is an unlimited hydroplane. Do you know what that means?"

"I suppose it means that she is very fast."

"She's fast, all right. She's fast enough to kill us and save Forster the trouble."

Karinovsky looked interested. "What speed will she attain?"

"She might have done 170 or 180 when she was new. But in her present beat-up condition, I doubt if she'll do much better than 130 or so."

"Kilometers or miles?"

"Miles per hour. In the dead of night with an Albanian chart across a bathtub-sized lagoon with more sandbars than water."

"I know nothing about boats," Karinovsky announced airily. "Besides—do we have any choice?"

We didn't, of course. Not really. Karinovsky was in no shape to swim across the Lagoon. There was no time to find another boat, and land transport was out. We were stuck with this shark-headed beast of a hydroplane. I would just have to take it slow and easy, and hope that I could manage without blowing it up or flipping it over, or grounding in the middle of the lagoon.

"All right," I said. "Cast off the line."

Karinovsky untied the boat and pushed it away from the dock. I turned on the ignition switch and kicked the starter.

The engine whined, then caught. The twelve pistons of the modified Merlin rumbled like an avalanche, and the exhaust sounded like a runaway machine gun.

"Can't you make it any quieter?" Karinovsky shouted. "We'll wake up the whole damned city."

"She's just idling now," I shouted back. "Hang on!"

And so it was that Agent X—demon driver of the world's fastest machines—settled back firmly against the headrest. There was a hard tight smile on his tanned hawk features, and his blunt skillful powerful hands rested lightly on the controls. With the delicacy of a surgeon he engaged the clutch and applied a touch of throttle.

The hydroplane responded with a roar that could probably be heard in Switzerland. The rpm indicator jumped to three thousand. The hydroplane shot forward like a shell from a cannon, and Agent X held on for dear life.

18

Several things were going wrong simultaneously. The hydroplane was traveling much too fast, and her bow was swinging hard to the left. I turned the steering wheel and the boat swung instantly to the right. Her starboard rail dipped, and the bow tried to dig itself into the water.

"Slow down!" Karinovsky screamed at me.

That was just what I was trying to do. I had taken my foot off the throttle, but it seemed to be jammed, we were still gaining speed. The tachometer had gone to 3,700. The boat, swinging again to the left, apparently was trying to run itself up on the causeway.

Again I turned the wheel to the right. Again the bow dug in, and the stern began to lift. It kept on lifting, and I threw in the clutch. The engine, spinning without any load, sounded as if it were flying apart. Then the throttle popped up, and the engine quieted down to an ear-shattering rumble. The boat settled down and grudgingly began to lose speed.

"What were you trying to do?" Karinovsky asked.

"The throttle jammed," I told him. "Also there's something wrong with the trim or something. She pulls to the left and tries to put her nose under on the right."

Karinovsky sighed and rubbed his face. "Perhaps I can operate the throttle for you."

"No, I need you to navigate. Where am I supposed to go?"

Karinovsky consulted the chart. "Straight down the main channel."

"But where in hell *is* the main channel?" I shouted.

"Don't get so nervous," Karinovsky said. "I think we follow that row of stakes over there."

"They look like fishing stakes."

"Quite possibly . . . . In that case, we steer by that big triangular thing over to the right."

"OK," I said. "Keep looking for more like it." I touched the throttle gently. Nothing happened. I applied a slow and even pressure. The throttle suddenly plunged to the floor and the hydroplane spurted ahead. I got my toe under the throttle and lifted. It returned to idling position and the boat eased down. We had already passed the marker, and another was coming up fast.

I repeated the operation, putting the throttle in and pulling it out with my toe. It sounded as if I were firing an 88-millimeter cannon. If they couldn't hear me in Switzerland, it was only because they weren't paying any attention. The hydroplane jumped forward in a series of nervous bows and curtsies, like a spastic Morris dancer. I could feel the drive shaft buckle and moan under the torque. I expected it to come apart any time at all.

"And now," Karinovsky said, "I believe we turn to the right."

The lights of the airport dock were bright in front of us. "Where to the right?" I asked.

"Just right, along the channel to Mazzorbo."

"What channel, you idiot? Where is it?"

"I believe you follow those stakes," Karinovsky said with dignity.

He pointed, and I saw a veritable forest of stakes to the right. Some of them might have been channel markers; the rest probably marked fishing areas, sandbars, crab traps or even buried treasure. I had no way of telling one type of stake from another. I would have to charge blindly through them, and hope that the tide was still high enough to get us over the sandbars.

I kept the engine idling and let the boat drift gently into the stakes. I picked a careful route among the larger stakes, passed as near them as possible, and hoped for the best.

I promptly ran aground.

"What do we do now?" Karinovsky asked.

"We get out and push," I told him.

"I hope it doesn't take long," Karinovsky said, following me over the side into waist-deep water. "We seem to have company coming."

I looked back toward Venice. One light low against the shoreline had detached itself and was moving towards us.

"Maybe it's a police launch," I said.

"Would you care to bet on it?"

"No, thanks. Get your shoulder under the bow. Lift when I do."

We strained against the heavy hull, our feet

sinking ankle-deep into the mud. The detached light had started moving near the Ospitale Umberto I. It was not traveling very fast—ten to fifteen miles an hour, I estimated—but it was coming steadily toward us.

The bow came free and the hydroplane slid backwards into four feet of water. We scrambled aboard. I looked around hastily for anything resembling a channel, found nothing, and put in the clutch and throttle. We thundered away to the east. Working the throttle carefully, I got us past San Michele and Murano, gaining distance easily on our pursuer. We were almost parallel to San Giacomo in Palude before we ran aground again.

It took longer to slide the hydroplane off this time. Our pursuer became visible as a low-powered launch of extremely shallow draft, coming for us across the flats. He closed the gap to about fifty yards, and I heard shots as I put in the throttle.

Then we thundered away again, throwing up a great curtain of white spray between us and our pursuer and making enough noise to scare the guards on the Yugoslav border. I bobbed and weaved through the stakes, knocking down any that didn't get out of my way fast enough, and praying that I wouldn't take a chunk of wood in the propeller.

We appraoched Mazzorbo, gaining easily on the launch, and Karinovsky hit me on the arm and shouted for a left turn. I followed instructions and ran aground again.

"It's hopeless," Karinovsky said. "We'd better swim to Mazzorbo."

"Wade, you mean. Anyhow, we'd never make it."

The launch was closing the distance; its occupants had begun firing again. I said, "Get up on the stern."

"What are you going to do?"

"Either back her off or blow her up," I told him. He nodded sadly and scrambled onto the stern. I climbed into the cockpit and put the clutch into reverse. Karinovsky's weight might lift the bow enough to get us off. Or it might not. I stamped on the throttle.

The Rolls-Royce engine howled like a wounded dinosaur. A ton of water was sucked up by the propeller and spewed into the air. The operator of the motor launch might have thought we were blowing up; I thought so myself. He sheered off abruptly, slowed, and lost way for a few moments before turning back toward us. I couldn't hear their guns above the engine, but I saw two starred holes appear in the safety glass of the windshield. Another bullet smashed into the instrument panel, obliterating the fuel gauge. The tachometer was still working, showing 5,000 rpms with the needle deep in the red. It was probably a matter of seconds before the engine tore off its mounts and exploded through the cowling.

Then the hydroplane slid off the bar and began to pick up speed backwards. Karinovsky, hanging on to a cleat with his good hand, was nearly thrown off. I shifted to neutral, dragged him into the cockpit, and shifted again.

There was no time for anything fancy. The next sandbar was going to be our last, anyhow.

I put the throttle to the floor and pointed the hydroplane at Palude del Monte.

It wasn't a bad way to go, if you really had to go. The supercharger screamed, and the heavy pistons tried to punch through their cylinders. The hydroplane climbed out of the water, balancing on her two sponsons and the bottom edge of her propeller. The bow trembled, trying to go airborne. I saw the long, hazy edge of a sandbar ahead. I drove straight into it, and the hydroplane hurdled the bar and flew like a bird. The propeller chewed on nothing, and the tachometer tried to bend itself around the limit peg. Then we hit water, bounced into the air again, hit and bounced, and then leveled off. We had made it. The shore was dead ahead of us, and I tried to get my foot under the accelerator.

I wasn't fast enough.

The supercharger chose that moment to come unglued. Spinning six times faster than the engine's crankshaft, the impeller simply disintegrated. The quill shaft between engine and supercharger flew apart, and the main shaft followed. The engine, spinning free, began to throw pistons, punching them through the engine. Chunks of ragged metal exploded through the cowling. The propeller joined in the fun and began shedding blades.

The hydroplane continued to move at a barely diminished speed.

We left the water and drove onto a marshy beach. The hydroplane didn't seem to notice that we were on land. It continued to race across the gray mud, discarding parts of its engine as it went. It ran out of beach and slid across a narrow road and into a grassy meadow. It was still bouncing and sliding at breakneck speed when it came to an unplowed field.

Without hesitation it pointed itself at a clump of trees. A big cedar struck it on the side, sending it into a flat spin. The hydroplane began to lose heart. It covered another twenty yards. A stretch of rock tore out what was left of its bottom, and it scored its final triumph by knocking over a medium-sized willow. Then it faltered and came to a final and unequivocal stop.

19

"We made it," I said, for want of anything better to say. Karinovsky did not reply. His eyes were closed, and his head was rolled back at an unnatural angle. I was struck by the terrible fear that all my brilliant aquabatics had been in vain. The operation had been a success, but the patient had died.

I lifted Karinovsky's head. Carefully, with a thumb and forefinger, I peeled back an eyelid.

"Will you kindly get your thumb out of my eye?" Karinovsky said.

"I thought you were dead."

"Even dead, I would not wish to be blinded," Karinovsky said. He raised himself and gazed thoughtfully at the Lagoon, some fifty or so yards behind us. Then he looked at the solid ground on all sides of our hydroplane. "Nye," he said, "I have suspected that you were a genius. But my words are pallid beside the splendor of your deed."

"It wasn't anything much," I told him. "Any psychotic could have done it."

"Perhaps. But *you* did it, my friend. You snatched us out of the closing jaws of the enemy. I hope now that you will reserve your modesty for those gullible enough to believe it."

"All right," I said. "But I could have saved us a hell of a lot easier in a rowboat."

"To be sure, Guesci might have chosen a more suitable craft. But a rowboat would have offended his artistic soul."

"Anyhow, we've made it to the mainland."

"Yes. But we are not out of reach of the enemy just yet."

"I suppose not. That launch must have landed by now."

"Also, there are Forster's land units to consider," Karinovsky said. "We must leave this coast as quickly as possible."

I had a vision of an eternal chase, endlessly protracted. We had come free of the labyrinth of Venice only to enter the great maze of the world. We were toy figures, doomed to keep our fixed positions in this particular dance of destiny, our bodies strained into conventional postures of flight.

"When will we be safe?" I asked.

"Soon," Karinovsky said, "when we have reached San Stefano di Cadore."

"Where in hell is that?"

"In the north of the Veneto, near Austria's Carinthian border, in the foothills of the Carnic Alps."

"Spare me geography," I said. "How far away is it?"

"A little less than a hundred kilometers."

"And how do we propose to get there?"

"Guesci has arranged it."

"Like he arranged the hydroplane? Listen, I don't—"

"Wait. Someone is coming."

I could make out a dark figure running silently toward us from the far side of the field. I plunged into the hydroplane's cockpit and found Karinovsky's revolver. Crouching, I rested the barrel against my left forearm, leading the target slightly. There was no wind.

Karinovsky put a hand on my wrist. "Don't be so impetuous," he said. "An attacker would not come so openly."

I held fire, but I kept the gun ready. After a boat-ride like this one I had just had, I wanted no trouble from anyone. I was prepared to go to considerable lengths to make my position clear.

The figure reached the side of our smashed hydroplane. There was an odor of sweat and garlic. Two hands reached out and gripped my shoulders.

"You were magnificent!" Guesci cried.

Dressed in a dark suit, with a black silk scarf knotted carelessly around his neck, and black kidskin gloves on his hands, Marcantonio Guesci clasped me to his breast and breathed heavy waves of appreciation in my face.

"I watched everything!" Guesci said. "From the moment you left the Sacca di San Girolamo I had you fixed in my binoculars."

"That helped a lot," I said, disengaging myself.

"Ah, but you needed no help. The speed at

which you crossed the Lagoon—"

"—was inadvertent," I said. "But I don't suppose you had much trouble finding us."

"About as much trouble as I would have in locating a forest fire," Guesci said. "One might wish that you had made a little less noise in your approach."

"One didn't have time to install a muffler," I told him.

"It *was* a noisy boat," Guesci admitted. "But all of that is behind us now. You and Mr. Karinovsky are practically safe."

"Practically?"

"Well, of course, we must still extricate ourselves from the Veneto coast. But that is a mere technical consideration. We have outfoxed Forster at every turn, and we shall outfox him now for the final time. Come, we go this way."

I was worried about Karinovsky. His arm had taken a considerable beating in the boat, and the wound had reopened. A slow trickle of blood was beginning to drip from his fingers. We had to support him as we moved away from the boat. I didn't think he was up to much more helling around.

"How are we going to outfox Forster this time?" I asked.

"We are going to do it—magnificently!" Guesci said. "To appreciate the plan, you must first consider our position."

"I've already considered it."

"Not fully. You know of the motor launch which is moving in behind us. But perhaps you do not know of Forster's other dispositions."

I knew not, neither did I care. But there was

no avoiding a majestic flow of extraneous information. We trudged through wet grass while Guesci (heir to the Borgias, poor man's Fu Manchu) outlined the position.

"Forster had to assume that you might escape from Venice; it was the only practical assumption to make with a man of your calibre. Therefore he set up a secondary line of defense, centering it on the Venezia-Mestre Causeway. His deployment to the south of the causeway, along the line Chioggia-Mestre, does not concern us; we are no longer in that theatre of war, so to speak. But on the northern front, tangential to the line Mestre-San Dona di Piave, our war is very active indeed. Consider, if you will, the main topographical features of our battlefield—"

"Guesci," I asked, "couldn't we skip all of this until later?" But my plea went unnoticed. General Guesci was showing his staff that amazing grasp of terrain so necessary in an intuitive and unorthodox commander of fighting men.

"The following features present themselves to our attention," Guesci said, metamorphosing smoothly into a brilliant instructor of tactics at military college. "We find ourselves on a square of land roughly 25 miles to a side, whose geographic homogeneity is maintained by the Venetian Lagoon to the south, the Alpine foothills to the north, the river Brenta to the west, and the Piave to the east. Within this operational area, moving northward from the Lagoon, Forster will guard the one arterial road which runs between Mestre and San Dona di Piave, plus the network of five secondary roads connecting the towns of Cazori, Compalto and Cercato. There is also a railroad, but this he can ignore since no train is due for another 30 hours. Thus, his arrangement has us hemmed in tightly between the Lagoon and the coastal highway. Viewed as a set piece, this scheme might seem irresistible."

"It does sound pretty good," I said. "How do we get out of it?"

Guesci had no intention of telling me just then. He continued to lead us across marsh and thin woods and stubbled fields, and he continued to explain the position.

"So that is the problem with which I was confronted," he said, sounding a little like C. Aubrey Smith in *Four Feathers,* only much sillier. "I considered the possibilities. It seemed to me that Northforce would be stretched very thin along the Mestre-San Dona line. Accordingly, I contemplated finding a vulnerable salient, and risking everything on a surprise breakthrough."

"Good!" Karinovsky said. "I approve. And I suggest that we—"

"But I rejected that scheme as quixotic," Guesci continued. "I had to assume that Forster was in radio contact with Southforce, and that, as soon as our position was pinpointed, those men would be moved by fast automobile to prearranged positions above the coastal road. In short, I had to consider Southforce as a highly mobile reserve. That left me with essentially the original position: men from the launch behind us, acting as beaters or as one arm of a pincer, moving to crush us against Forster's reinforced line. Do I make myself clear?"

"Marvellously clear," I said. "You've thought out the situation beautifully."

Guesci beamed with pleasure. "Above all, I did not wish to underestimate the enemy."

"No one could accuse you of that," I said. "You figured every aspect of the trap; unfortunately we are still in the middle of it."

"I realize that," Guesci said, with an air of insufferable subtlety. "It is exactly what I planned. Consider: Forster lays a trap for us and expects us to try to avoid it, thus exposing ourselves to even greater risks. But we take an immediate initiative by stepping into the center of the snare—the one place he would never expect to find us!"

"OK, so we've outsmarted him again. But what are we going to do?"

"We shall escape."

"How?"

"By proceeding to those haystacks in the field ahead." Guesci shot back his cuff and frowned at his watch in a professional manner. "If I have calculated correctly we should be surrounded at that point, with men closing in from all sides." He smirked. "But we will have perhaps a little surprise for them."

It was too much. I grabbed the little sadist and shook him until I could hear the coins jingle in his pocket. I shoved my wolf's muzzle into his startled face, bared my fangs, and said, "You quick-talking little son of a bitch, if you've got a way out of this I want to hear it now, immediately."

Guesci said, "Please do not crush my jacket." I released him, and he brushed himself off. "Come this way," he said. I had to admire him, even if he was going to get us all killed.

We crossed the field and came to the three large haystacks. Guesci waved his hand negligently at the center stack.

"Behold!"

I stared. Guesci, grinning like a hyena, walked up to the stack and began to pull away armfuls of hay. A long dark shape was revealed underneath. He cleared away more hay. I looked, and was momentarily incapable of words.

"Guesci," I said at last, "I take back my unkind words. Maybe you are a genius."

Standing before us, bright with promise, strewn with loose hay like the freshly unpacked toy of a giant, was a high-wing monoplane. Its wingtips and tail were still obscured, but the shapely curve of its propeller spoke of freedom. I helped Guesci finish the clearing, then stood back in admiration.

"Beautiful, is it not?" Guesci said. "While the mad dogs slink toward us over the ground, we soar deliciously away; we leave them howling and gnashing their teeth at the moon."

"The device is worthy of you, my friend," I said, falling into Guesci's style through sheer gratitude. "Our destination is San Stefano?"

"Correct. There is no airport, but I have selected several areas as suitable for a light craft such as this. Colonel Baker and his men await us there. The trip should take no more than an hour."

There was a gray hint of dawn in the east, and I saw movement on two sides of the field. A dog barked; there was a sound of metal striking bone, and the dog was abruptly silent.

"The pack is closing in," Guesci said, smiling.

"My dear friend, shall we make our departure?"

"That," I said giddily, "is a suggestion with which I am in accord. Karinovsky, are you all right?"

"Well enough," Karinovsky said. "I am merely standing here and bleeding to death while you two have your fun."

"We'll fix you up in the plane," I said. "Let's go."

We helped Karinovsky into the small cabin and strapped him securely into a seat. Dawn was coming up fast; crouching shapes were moving toward us across the field. I started to climb into the copilot's seat, and found that Guesci was already there.

"You're in the wrong seat," I told him.

"No, I'm not," he said.

"Guesci," I said, "this is no time for jokes. They're coming. You'd better move over and get us out of here."

"What are you talking about?" Guesci asked, his voice going shrill. "I know nothing about aircraft! Nothing! *You* must get us out of here!"

"Look," I said, "You arranged this whole stupid plane thing!"

"But I arranged it for you," Guesci said, sounding on the verge of tears. "Mr. Nye, please, it is well known that you are an expert in the operation of all types of aircraft. You are famous for it! In the name of God! Why else would I get a plane?"

It had happened again. The famous and highly skilled Agent X—that damned super-specter, my dark alter ego—had risen again to haunt me, betray me, destroy me. Agent X—that compulsive player of bizarre and inhuman games, the killer within the law, madman by government approval—how I detested him, and how greatly he must have hated me. But now, my saturnine and certifiable twin had finally found a way to kill his deadliest adversary—myself.

Guesci was tugging at my arm. He pulled me into the pilot's seat, and I looked at the unfamiliar array of instruments. I was touched by a black moment of calm in which I realized that the fault was entirely my own. Agent X was no more than a label for an impulse; and Guesci—well, I should have known that a man who arranges escapes by scuba and hydroplane might reasonably be expected to have an airplane tucked away somewhere.

"Nye!" Guesci said. "They're coming! Take us out of here."

I smiled slowly, sadly. "Karinovsky," I called out, "can you fly a plane?"

"I do not think so," Karinovsky said. "I have never tried."

I could count eight crouching men on the edges of the field. They were moving slowly, with extreme caution—but they were coming.

20

I had exaggerated slightly. My acquaintance with light aircraft was surely deficient, but not entirely lacking. For example, I had flown as a passenger upon several occasions. I had once been given the controls of a Piper Cub float plane; in level flight, I had performed a series of gently banked turns with credible skill. And finally, I had seen innumerable airplane movies.

This, obviously, was insufficient experience for the job ahead of me. But I had even less experience in my only alternative course of action: crossing an open field at dawn under the guns of eight or more men. Necessity forced my choice; I turned to the instrument panel.

I found the battery switch and turned it on. Just under the panel to my right was the fuel shutoff valve. I turned this on, and found the carburetor-heat control. It was marked "Pull for Hot." I did so. Then I turned the mixture control to "Full-Rich."

"What are you doing?" Guesci asked.

"I'm getting ready to fly us out of here."

"Oh." Guesci thought for a moment. "But I thought you didn't know how to fly."

"I don't. But this seems as good a time to learn as any."

"I suppose it is," Guesci said, laughing uncertainly. "But may I urgently request that you hurry?"

I nodded. My feet were resting on two pedals, but I couldn't remember what they were for. Brakes? No. Surely not two brake pedals. I pressed the right one and heard a soft creak from the rear of the plane. I leaned out the window and saw that the rudder had turned. Very well; pedals controlled rudder. I remembered that the stick in front of me operated the ailerons and elevators.

Now what? There were instruments showing altitude, direction, elapsed time, oil temperature, fuel supply, oil pressure, and engine rpms. There was a bewildering array of switches and dials, many of them with printed instructions or warnings. I read these quickly, trying to remember what I had heard about takeoff procedure. It seemed to me—

I became aware that Guesci was pounding me on the arm.

"What's the matter?" I asked.

"They are firing at us!" Guesci said. "Can't you hear it?"

I could, now that he mentioned it. Forster's men were still at a fair distance from us, but they were within pistol range. There was no more time to brood over the mysteries of flight. It was time now to do or die; or to do *and* die, as seemed more likely.

"Here we go," I said, and pressed the started button.

Nothing happened.

I stabbed at the button repeatedly, got no reaction, and searched the instrument panel for a clue to the failure. I found something called the "Magneto Switch." It had four positions—Off, L, R, Both. I switched it to "Both," and pressed the starter button again.

The engine coughed, complained, and came to life with a roar. I held the stick in what I hoped was a neutral position, rested my feet lightly on the pedals, and watched the tachometer and oil pressure climb. The plane trembled but did not move.

I advanced the throttle, and the tachometer went to 2,400 rpm. Above that was a red-marked danger zone. The plane quivered like a willow in a windstorm, but did not move.

Then I noticed the hand brake. I closed the throttle to an idle and released the brake.

We began to roll, our speed increasing rapidly as I opened the throttle.

I remembered that a plane was supposed to take off into the wind. But I didn't know if there was any wind; and if there was, I didn't know what I could do about it now. I also remembered that a plane had to be traveling quite rapidly before it would leave the ground. Therefore I slammed the throttle to the firewall, in a maneuver I had learned from Real Air Aces. (This would also have been the moment to cut in the afterburner, if I had had one.)

We must have been doing 50 miles an hour over the ground, though the airspeed indicator showed 20. Alarmingly, the plane was beginning to swing to the right. I touched the right pedal, found that the swing was accentuated, and quickly pressed the left pedal. The plane straightened for a moment, then began to turn left. I compensated again.

We were rushing along at 60 or so miles an hour. There was a low stone wall ahead, and trees beyond it. The plane was barely under my control. I was trying to work the pedals lightly, but I must have been overcompensating. We advanced in a series of long S-turns.

The stone wall was coming up fast now. In the rear, Karinovsky was utterly silent. Guesci had begun to whimper, and buried his face in his arms. I resisted the impulse to do the same. I reached out to pull the throttle fully open, and found it already was fully open. So I pulled the stick back toward my lap as I had seen countless pilots do in countless movies.

The plane left the ground and soared into the air, exactly as a plane is supposed to do. I hadn't really believed it would happen; but I could see the ground falling away, and we were climbing into a cloudless dawn sky of faint blue. The engine had taken on a querulous note of strain, and the tachometer had fallen to 1,900 rpms. I eased the stick forward, letting the plane climb at a more gradual angle.

Guesci was saying something to me, but I wasn't listening. I was filled with the sensation of accomplishment. I had gotten this airplane into the air! I was by God flying!

It was a moment of personal triumph, to be savored as long as possible. I decided not to concern myself just now with the interesting problem of how or in what condition I would get down to earth again. *One thing at a time:* that is the only motto for a soldier of fortune, especially if he is somewhat inclined toward hysteria.

21

The takeoff had been frightening, but exhilarating. As we soared gloriously into the blue, I had come to the conclusion that flying was not so terribly difficult after all; that it was, in fact, a skill that any reasonably bright man could perform by the concentrated application of his intellect. It seemed to me that the professionals had made a mystery cult out of this essentially simple operation for much too long; they had been guarding their livelihoods with calculated guile.

There was an alternative possibility: that flying *was* in fact extremely difficult, but that I was just one of those seat-of-the-pants naturals who instinctively do everything right.

Some moments later I had rejected both explanations. I knew that I had gotten the plane into the air through sheer luck, aided by the craft's built-in tendency to do the right thing whenever possible.

This insight came to me very suddenly, when

the plane turned sharply to the left for no apparent reason.

We were still climbing. The tachometer showed 2,300 rpms, the stick was back, and my feet were resting lightly on the rudder pedals. The airspeed indicator showed 50 miles per hour —dangerously close to the indicated stalling speed of 40. The altimeter gave me 500 feet; too close to the ground, but we were still gaining altitude.

And then we were turning to the left for no reason whatsoever.

I pushed down gently on the right rudder pedal. The plane straightened, but the airspeed fell to 45. The engine sounded unhappy. I tried to feed more gas, but the throttle was wide open. We skidded into a flat right turn and the engine stalled momentarily. In a panic I kicked the left pedal and pushed the stick forward. The plane's nose dropped toward the horizon and the airspeed increased to 60; but the rpms edged up to the red line, and the plane turned hard to the left, and I suddenly needed four hands and at least two heads.

I corrected the turn and pulled back gently on the stick. The rpms fell to a safe level as soon as the plane started to climb; but of course, the airspeed dropped again toward a stall. I moved the stick carefully, forward and then backward, until I found a point where rpms and airspeed were both in the black. The plane was climbing very shallowly. I had to keep using left rudder to keep a straight course, and this worried me. But for the moment everything was nicely balanced.

"What happened?" Guesci asked, his voice trembling.

"Bit of rough air," I told him. No sense in alarming the passengers; there was no room on this plane for anyone's panic but my own.

"But you really do know how to fly, don't you?" he asked. "I mean, you were joking earlier and you really do know how to fly, don't you?" His whining voice irritated me.

"You can see for yourself," I said brusquely, correcting for a left turn and easing the stick forward to stop a stall and reducing engine speed somewhat to keep the tachometer out of the red and then correcting for a left turn again.

"You seem to be having trouble," he said.

"Look," I told him, "it takes time to adjust to a crate like this after you're used to a Mach 2 fighter." I swear, I hardly knew what I was saying.

Guesci nodded vehemently. He wanted to believe in my skill, despite a certain amount of evidence to the contrary. There are no atheists in foxholes, especially when the foxhole is a thousand or so feet above northern Italy.

"You have had much experience with jet fighters?" he asked.

"Mostly with Sabres and Banshees," I said, correcting for a left turn and easing the stick forward to prevent a stall and reducing engine speed, etc. "Did I ever tell you about the time I had a flameout over Chosin Reservoir?"

"No—Was it very bad?"

"Well, I suppose it was kinda hairy," I said, and bit my lip to keep from giggling. Then my attention was taken up by the plane, which needed correcting for a left turn and simultaneously easing of the stick forward to prevent a stall and then reducing engine speed, etc., etc.

When I had completed this, I told Guesci to take care of Karinovsky. Then I sternly rid myself of all notions of frivolity and concentrated on the serious task of trying to outguess the airplane.

We were doing 105 miles an hour, and somehow we had climbed to 3,000 feet. I closed the throttle to the indicated cruise-setting, and the airspeed dropped and held at 90. The compass had us traveling nearly southwest. It was full dawn now, and the gleaming, wrinkled hide of the Adriatic was below me. Tolmezzo, our destination, was in the Alps, which meant somewhere in the north. I moved the stick gently to the right.

The plane responded by dipping her right wing. Her nose lifted at the same time, and her airspeed began to fall. I was sure that the damned engine was about to quit on me, and I pulled the stick abruptly back.

It was the wrong move. The plane rolled, the engine coughed like a wounded panther, and the nose came up alarmingly. I gave full power (slamming the throttle to the firewall) and corrected with left rudder and stick.

The plane rolled, I corrected again, and the distant line of the horizon teetered back and forth. My airspeed had fallen to 60.

I realized at last that I should have pushed the stick *forward,* not back. I did so now, dove, regained airspeed, and found my right wing slanting toward the sea.

I corrected, and the right wing came up and the left wing snapped down. Guesci was shouting at me, and Karinovsky had been roused from the contemplation of his wound.

We were in trouble. Each time I corrected, the plane rolled more deeply to the other side. I could feel a heavy vibration in the tail, and we had somehow dropped to 990 feet and were still falling. I couldn't seem to straighten the plane out; she seemed determined to flip herself over or tear off a wing.

Then Guesci made a lunge for the controls, and I fought him off, and Karinovsky was shouting at both of us. Guesci and I clawed and grunted at each other, and Guesci tried to bite my wrist, and I hit him on the nose with my forehead. That calmed him down.

During this time, no one had been flying the plane. I turned quickly to the controls and found that we were no longer rolling. With my hand removed from the helm, the plane had quietly corrected herself. She was descending now, and making a wide turn to the right.

I had learned an extremely valuable lesson: when in doubt, let the plane do it.

I worked the stick carefully, trying to let the plane fly itself. I got us up to 4,000 feet, traveling slightly east of north at 95 miles an hour. The plane kept itself in level flight with very little help from me. When everything seemed in order, I turned to Guesci.

"Don't ever do that again," I said, in a cold, hard voice.

"I'm terribly sorry," Guesci said. "I didn't understand what you were doing."

Karinovsky said, "He was testing the responses of the aircraft. Any fool could see that."

"Of course, of course, I realize that now," Guesci said.

There is no greater marvel on earth than the will to believe. Even I was starting to believe.

"Mr. Nye," Guesci said, "I am truly sorry. . . . Will you have to do any more testing?"

"That," I said, "depends on conditions."

Guesci nodded. Karinovsky didn't even bother to nod; it was obvious that one tested according to conditions.

"How do conditions seem?" Guesci asked timidly.

I thought for a while before answering. I had a splitting headache, and my clothes were drenched with perspiration. I had acquired a pronounced tic in the right eye, and there was a tremor to my hands reminiscent of the early stages of locomotor ataxia. But the main fact was that I was still flying the plane.

"Conditions are not bad," I told him. "In fact, at the moment, everything is very much in order."

How does the fool build his paradise?—out of the crumbling bricks of illusion and the watery cement of hope. Thus spake Zarathustra Nye.

22

We had flown to the northeast for nearly 15 minutes. The Adriatic was behind us, and the wide North Italian plain was below. I decided that it was time to find out where we were going. I asked Guesci if we had any maps.

"Of course," Guesci said. "I provided everything." He reached under the seat and brought out a chart numbered ONC-F-2. It showed northern Italy and most of middle Europe, and it was filled with symbols for airports, DF stations, restricted areas, cities, towns, mountains, swamps, oceans, lakes, power lines, dams, bridges, tunnels, and many other interesting features. It bore absolutely no resemblance to the flat green and brown land beneath us.

I decided to delegate responsibility. "Guesci," I said, "find out where we are. Then find out where we should be, and how we get there."

"But I know nothing of aerial maps!" Guesci said.

"Karinovsky will help you. After all, you can't expect me to do everything."

They went to work on the map. I used the time trying to learn something about flying an airplane. I performed gentle banks to the right and left, dove, climbed, tried different throttle settings, and experimented with the trim. I began to feel a modest sensation of confidence.

"Would you mind flying a little lower?" Guesci asked. "I can't seem to find any landmark."

I brought the plane down to 2,000 feet. After a while, Guesci sighed and said, "The countryside around here is featureless."

"You're a great help," I said.

Guesci had been studying the map. Now he asked, "How long has it been since we left the Adriatic and crossed the coast?"

"About 17 minutes, I'd guess."

"At what speed and direction?"

"About 90 miles an hour, northeast. But that's only an estimate."

Karinovsky waved his hand negligently. "We'll call it a hundred miles an hour, since it makes the calculation easier. That means we have traveled approximately 25 miles. Continuing to the north, we shall soon intersect the Piave River. It is a landmark we are not likely to miss."

"What do we do when we find it?"

"We then follow it. It will bring us to Belluno, and then we can follow the Piave valley all the way to San Stefano di Cadore."

"How will we know when we get there?"

Guesci had the answer to that one. "There is

a power station just before the town."

"Are you sure you can find it?"

"Don't worry," Guesci said. "You take care of the piloting, and we will handle the navigating."

Somehow I didn't like the sound of that; but of course, there was nothing to do but bash on.

I continued to the north, and soon we spotted the Piave. I turned the plane and followed the course of the river to the northwest, past a double loop, and then a second one. We checked out our position on Valdobbiadene. The ground was beginning to rise now, and I had to keep the plane in a gentle climb.

In a few minutes we came into the foothills of the Alps, about 2,000 feet above sea level. The river turned north, and then northeast. Guesci spotted the town of Feltre on our left, and Karinovsky located a windmill on the right. Everything checked out nicely. We were 9,000 feet above sea level by the time we reached Belluno. The Alps stretched in front of us like massed spear-points. It was getting cold in the cabin.

The plane was harder to control now. Strong updrafts buffeted the wings, and the engine labored in the thin air. Below us, the valley of the Piave was a distinct curving slash through the Dolomites. The upward trend of the land forced me to 10,000 feet.

I heard Karinovsky gasp. Turning, I saw the peak of a mountain slide by a hundred yards to my right. It towered at least a quarter of a mile above our present elevation.

"Any more around like that?" I asked.

"Nothing else to worry about at this altitude,"

Karinovsky said. "Unless we miss San Stefano."

The Piave valley continued to curve to the east, and Guesci spotted the last power station. Then we saw San Stefano to the right, at an elevation of 8,481 feet. I banked and began a gentle descent.

Individual houses came into focus. There were steeply tilted little meadows, and a single-track railroad cut through one edge of the town.

"There is our destination!" Guesci cried.

I saw the lodge, U-shaped, set about a mile from the village. There was a stretch of open land in front of the U; from the air it looked about the size of a postage stamp. I couldn't possibly land on anything so small, of course; but I didn't see anything else that looked any better. I continued to let down, circling the field and hoping that it wouldn't be so bad as it looked.

I circled the field, trying to get myself near the edge of the field with the aircraft facing into the wind. I reduced speed and eased the stick forward. A cluster of trees flashed by, the lodge shot past, and then I was at the far end of the field, turning into the northeast wind.

It had all happened too fast. Suddenly I was very near the ground, traveling at a terrifying speed, too low for safety but too high for a landing. According to what I had learned from Smilin' Jack and his friends, I should apply power, regain altitude, and make my approach again. But I didn't dare. My control of the plane was too tentative, and the ground looked too close. I gritted my teeth and shoved the stick forward, at the same time slamming the throttle shut.

Fifteen feet or so above the ground the plane faltered, lost speed, and trembled on the verge of a dive. Half of the field had gone by. I pulled back hard on the stick. The plane dragged her nose into the air, shook indignantly, and came down hard on her tailwheel. Then the front wheels struck and the plane bounded high into the air. I kept the stick in my stomach and held on.

We came down hard. The left landing strut collapsed, and the plane fell heavily on her fuselage and began turning to the left. The left wingtip dug into the ground and the propeller struck and came apart. I shoved frantically on the right pedal and applied the brakes. The plane continued spinning around her left wingtip, rising into the air and trying to turn over. For a moment it looked as if she would make it. Then the right front strut collapsed, and the plane slid along sullenly on her belly. She came to a stop at the far end of the field, about 20 feet from a low wooden fence with pine woods beyond. I reached out and turned off the ignition. Agent X had struck again.

No one was hurt, but no one felt inclined to conversation. We surveyed the wreckage of the plane in silence, and then started walking to the lodge.

Already I was experiencing a sense of letdown. When I passed that wide oak door, the life of Agent X would be at an end. All that would be left would be that dubious quantity—William P. Nye. It seemed terribly unfair, and suddenly I wanted to turn and run from this alpine lodge, run from Italy, escape from Europe. I wanted to save myself by losing myself, to keep alive somehow that preposterous image of Agent X.

We were on the porch, and Guesci's hand reached out to the heavy bronze doorknob. I gave up my dream of flight and rebirth, and invented a proverb to fit the occasion: he who produces an illusion is more likely than anyone else to be taken in by it. The thought gave me very little comfort.

A young man with a crew cut opened the door and told us that we were expected. We entered, and walked down a short hall and into a large room with a picture window that overlooked the Alps.

A man was standing at the far end of the room, in front of a large fireplace, his hands clasped behind his back. Low flames cast his shadow across the ceiling. He turned slowly, smiling.

"Gentlemen," he said, "I am very glad that you made it. I was beginning to worry about you."

The man was Forster. He stood and smiled, standing erect but relaxed. Behind us, the door closed.

23

Tableau: the three bears meet wolfman. Yes, it was a moment to savor, if you like the taste of ashes in your mouth. The worst of it was remembering how hard I had worked to bring us to this particular place and no other. I hadn't even considered going somewhere else. It had never occurred to me that our destination might have been compromised. But here we were, and I felt that it was damned unfair. . . .

So *that* is how they play this game, I thought, maudlin with self-pity. You run and dodge and improvise and finally reach the desired sanctuary, only to find that the rules have been changed and the sanctuary has become the enemy stronghold and that you have actually lost.

But of course, I had forgotten: this game had no rules.

Meanwhile, back at the old reality, two men were covering us with revolvers while a third searched us. When that formality was over,

Forster invited us into the room. We entered like zombies, took the chairs he pointed to, and even accepted drinks and cigarettes. Forster's men faded back into the wings, and Forster stepped forward into a pink spotlight. We sat and stared at him; we were going to listen to whatever he had to say, and then we were going to let him shoot us. Moralewise, we were not a happy group.

"First," Forster said, "let me answer a question which you should be asking—what am I doing here instead of scrambling around in the Veneto marshes?"

We didn't say a word. Forster said, "I'll answer my own question. Guesci, your arrangements weren't quite so secret as you had thought. Your discreet inquiries concerning boats, aircraft, and the use of a lodge in San Stefano came to my attention. I left most of my men in Venice, to capture or kill you if possible, but failing that, to maintain pressure on you. There was no necessity for me to supervise so routine an operation. I came to San Stefano to await you, relying on your obstinacy to outweigh your intelligence. Naturally, I had to divert your people first. That was not too difficult. I sent them an emergency message from Guesci, changing the location of the meeting. Colonel Baker and his assistants are presently in Villa Santini, some 18 miles from here."

Forster waited for a reaction and got nothing. Our numbness annoyed him. He said, "I thought that a little chat with the three of you would be amusing; it turns out to be a bore. I suppose there is no reason to waste any more of my time."

Unhurriedly he drew a heavy Browning automatic from his jacket pocket. And just about that time, I came to the conclusion that I didn't want to die. I mean *really*. I wanted to live; for another 30 or 40 years, if possible, but at least for another 30 or 40 minutes if that was all I could get. I wanted to live badly enough to overcome the blissful stupor I had fallen into, to return to the possibilities of failure and pain. In order to live I was willing to crawl and beg, to lie and steal, to turn communist or federalist, Aryan or Orthodox, Aztec or Spaniard, or anything else the situation required.

I was even willing to become Agent X; and that, curiously, was the most difficult thing of all.

I said to Forster, "What happens now?"

He grinned. "Now I shoot you."

"In the back of the head?"

"Perhaps. Are you frightened, Mr. Nye?"

"Of course. But more than that, I'm disappointed."

"That is quite understandable. In your position—"

"You don't understand," I told him. "I'm disappointed in you."

"What are you talking about?" Forster asked.

"Your cowardice," Agent X replied.

I could feel his men lean forward almost imperceptibly. Forster raised his automatic and thumbed back the hammer.

"For that remark," he said, "you get it in the face."

"It makes no difference," I told him. "Your bullet won't alter the fact that I'm a better man dead than you are alive."

Forster was silent for a moment. Then he said, "Mr. Nye, you are trying to provoke me into some course of action which would give you a fighting opportunity. You are doing it rather clumsily, but the intent is clear. It is useless, of course. Our time of personal rivalry is over. I have a job to perform, and a duty to do it in the most efficient manner."

I stretched my stone mouth into a grin. "I expected you to hide behind your job, Forster. It's lucky you've got that gun. Otherwise I'd break you in two."

My bragging words were having an effect on him; not because they were true, but precisely because they weren't true. He knew he could take me, and it irritated him that circumstances would not allow him to prove it.

He said, "Your tactics do you credit, Mr. Nye. Still—what else could you say under present conditions?"

Very true; but Forster was speaking now for the benefit of his men. He was trying to convince them. He should have shot me three minutes ago and saved his explanations for later.

I said, "Your behavior might be understandable if you were some minor functionary. In that case, you wouldn't even consider matching yourself against me; it would be too ridiculous. But I had considered you a man like myself."

I paused to light a theatrical cigarette. I said, "We have had the same sort of career. But with a difference. I have achieved a certain modest fame as a fighter; you have acquired the reputation of a fairly competent bureaucrat."

Forster was too furious to speak. I was being most damnably unfair, of course; but I have always felt that dying was the unfairest thing of all.

"You have many good qualities," I told him. "You are clever, ruthless, and reasonably intelligent. Unfortunately, you lack the instinct for personal combat."

"You've said enough," Forster said.

"I'm sorry I had to tell you that. But surely it's better to hear it from me than from your employers."

"By God, that's enough!" Forster cried, raising his automatic.

"I think you should put me out of the way at once," I said quickly. "There are worse things I might tell you."

"You fantastic paranoid!" Forster shouted. "Do you really believe so much in your reputation?"

I forced myself to lean back and fold my arms. My dead mouth spasmed into a deprecating smile. "Forster," I said, "I could meet you with any weapons, at any time, under any circumstances, and kill you without undue effort. I could spot you a sword for a can opener and still take you apart without too much inconvenience. You should always let others do your fighting; otherwise some bad-tempered fellow is apt to kick your head off while you are fumbling with a safety catch."

One of Forster's men didn't quite conceal his smile. That was good; and what was better, Forster had noticed it.

Guesci and Karinovsky were staring at me

open-mouthed. I glanced at them, then turned back to Forster. "These cattle," I said, indicating my companions, "don't really matter at all. Guesci is the eternal amateur, and Karinovsky has very little importance in the overall picture. The contest was always between you and me. What do you think, Forster?"

He stood and glared at me. Then his face relaxed and his eyebrows lifted. He said slowly, "I believe that you are bluffing."

"Am I?"

"Yes, you are. Your words have a hollow ring—a desperate, cornered sound."

"You'll never know for sure," I said.

"I will know," Forster replied. He thumbed down the hammer of his Browning and put the gun in his pocket.

One of his men called out, "Excuse me, sir, it would be unwise to allow—"

"Shut up!" Forster said. "What is between Nye and me is not your concern. Nothing changes. If I fight with Nye and lose, you know what to do, don't you?"

The man nodded unwillingly.

Forster turned to me. "According to your dossier, you are quite an expert in antique armament. Is this true?"

"Try me."

"You will be tried. I also believe that you implied that you could kill me with any weapon?"

"Correct."

"Any weapon at all? You're quite sure?"

"Take your pick," I said, and realized that I had been drawn into a tactical error. Forster meant to kill me, but he wanted to do so on his own terms. The fight was for the edification of his men and, ultimately, for his superiors. It was designed to make Forster look good. In my eagerness to stretch out my time, I had been maneuvered into a position where I had to agree willingly to any weapon that Forster chose.

"I beg you to reconsider," Forster said, grinning amiably. He was making the trap iron-clad. No one would ever accuse him of forcing his own choice.

I decided to make it sound good. "I told you several times, Forster: any weapon. Do I have to put it in writing?"

"That won't be necessary," Forster said. "I just wanted to be sure I understood you. I think we can find an adequate selection of weapons in this room."

He gestured at the far wall. I got up from my chair and walked over to it. It was covered with cavalry sabres, broadswords, Pathan daggers, a nail-studded mace, a morning star, and other, less familiar items.

"Would you find these interesting?" Forster asked. He was pointing to a crossed set of scimitars, Turkish or Arabian by their look, with deeply curved blades.

"They'll do," I said.

"But perhaps they are not interesting enough," Forster said judiciously. "Let me see now—what do you think of the kris?"

I decided that he was trying to test my reaction to various weapons in order to find one which I was unfamiliar with. He could have spared himself the trouble; my knowledge of swordplay was confined to an early reading of

Sabatini and a remembrance of certain Errol Flynn movies.

"The kris is fine by me," I said.

"An overrated weapon," Forster said, moving down the wall. "These big, two-handed Crusader's swords are interesting, though clumsy."

"But potent enough in skilled hands," I said.

"Quite so. Have you ever handled a mace?"

"The principle seems clear enough."

"And what about this?"

I looked and hesitated for a fraction of a second too long. "Fine," I said quickly, trying to cover my mistake.

But Forster had caught it. He said, "If you don't object, these might afford us a measure of amusement."

He took down a short-handled double-headed axe with a leather thong through its handle. "Try the other one," he said. "See if you like it."

It was a thoroughly nasty weapon. The twin heads curved back in an exaggerated crescent. I tested the blades, and found them honed to razor sharpness.

"Viking, of course," Forster said. "A true berserker's weapon. Not as handy as the rapier, you might think; but you would be surprised. There is a technique to the use of the axe. The Viking axemen had little to fear from the swordsmen of their day. Take a shield, Nye; it's part of the equipment."

Again I had to hesitate, to let Forster pick a shield first from the dozen or so on the wall. Then I chose a similar one. It was a round, bronze-studded target with an arm-loop and a hand-grip. It was surprisingly light; I saw that it was made of heavy leather stretched over a wood frame, and reinforced with bronze.

"Shall we try ourselves with these?" Forster asked.

"Just as you wish."

"I warn you, I am not entirely unfamiliar with this weapon."

"It doesn't matter," I said, truthfully.

Forster turned to his men. "You will not interrupt this duel. If I lose, that is my own bad luck. If that should happen, you know what to do. Get rid of these three, and then get out of Italy."

He bowed to me. "I am at your service, Mr. Nye."

"All right," I said. Then I smiled. It was another bluff, designed to make Forster think that he might have tricked himself into the wrong choice of weapons. But the time for bluffs and counterbluffs had passed. Forster came toward me, blank-faced, his shield tilted forward, his axe arm cocked. Now I was fighting for whatever fractional part of my life was left to me.

24

We circled warily, shields outthrust and axe arms raised, with me taking up an inside position and Forster moving around me on springy legs. It occurred to me now, for the first time in several minutes, that I was really *not* Agent X, master of arms and stratagems, killer extraordinary and wizard of a thousand recourses. I was no more than William P. Nye, a pleasant, peaceable fellow who had somehow maneuvered himself into an axe duel with a large, angry, strongly built, quick-moving man who meant to kill me, and who would probably succeed.

Forster feinted and swung a quick blow. I jumped away from it, ready for a counterstroke. I had no chance for it. Forster's recovery was disconcertingly fast. The swing of the heavy axe hadn't overbalanced him; he had brought the weapon back into position instantly, with an impressive display of wrist. Then he was driving forward again.

I took two quick blows on my shield and swung side-arm, missed, and knew at once that I had put too much effort in the blow. I was unable to recover in time, and Forster's axe was coming down on my exposed arm.

I pushed forward as the blow fell, driving my right arm into Forster's chest, forcing him to miss. Forster jumped back at once, recovered beautifully, feinted with his shield and drove again. I was feinted out of position, but managed to block with my axe. I felt the shock run down my arm as our weapons clashed in midair.

I realized that I was losing this fight, just as I had expected to lose it. I was dismayed when I realized that. Agent X would certainly not *expect* to lose a fight.

Forster was coming at me again, feinting with both shield and axe. He was grinning; where had the bastard learned how to fight with an axe? I swung at him, he blocked, took a quick cut at my head, and then came back in a lunging backhand below my shield. I reacted too late; his axe slashed me across the left thigh.

The pain steadied me. I saw Karinovsky and Guesci sitting together on the couch, watching with grave faces. Forster's three men were on the far side of the room, their guns lowered, watching the battle with enjoyment. Suddenly, I wanted to win this fight. No matter what happened afterwards, I wanted to win now.

I lunged forward, catching Forster off-balance. I swung the axe like a man swatting flies, and Forster backed away, blocking a blow to the head, a blow to the waist, another blow to the head. Whenever I swung, Forster's axe or shield was there. Then he slipped a blow like a boxer, and swung underhand at my exposed right armpit.

No block was possible. I threw myself out of the way, and escaped with a long shallow wound down my ribs. We disengaged and began circling again.

So far, I was not doing very well. Forster was carving me up a little at a time, and I seemed incapable of doing anything about it. It was bad enough that he could handle an axe; what was worse was that he knew now that I couldn't.

Forster circled, feinting and recovering, moving in and out on spring-steel legs. I turned with him, the breath rasping in my throat, my right arm sagging under five or six pounds of steel. I could feel the strain clear down my back, and my left thigh was beginning to stiffen.

Forster chopped suddenly, scalloping a few inches from my shield. He pulled the axe head free and slashed backhanded, nearly taking off my left hand. I feinted and swung, and might have wounded him if there had been any strength left in my arm. I was learning; but not fast enough to do me much good. We exchanged blows, and I took a graze across the side before I could disengage and back away.

I still wanted to win this fight, but I knew that I wasn't going to. Not like this. Forster was going to dismember me, and without any particular effort. It was the sort of defeat that Agent X would never have stood for. Agent X had only one motto: win. The means weren't important, and fair and foul were interchangeable. The only thing was to win.

My only problem was how to accomplish this desirable objective.

It seemed to me that my chance lay with Forster. If he had simply wanted to kill me, he could have done so before now. But he didn't want it to end like that; he wanted to do it slowly. I would have to make an opportunity out of Forster's desire for an impressive performance.

He rushed again and I backed away, my mind made up. Forster chopped at me like a man breaking down a door, and I continued to retreat, tripped, and fell backward.

As I hit the floor, I tried to cover myself with the shield. My legs were exposed to a maiming blow, and Forster laughed and tapped me gently on the ankle.

"Do get up, Mr. Nye," he said. "You make it too easy for me." He backed away a few feet, just as I thought he would.

I stood up slowly, slipping my wrist out of the leather thong. Then I stepped backwards and feinted a backhanded throw at Forster's head. Forster raised his shield automatically, exposing his chest and belly. I swung forehand with everything left in me, releasing the axe at the peak of its swing.

Forster guessed what I was trying to do. With perfect reflex action he swung his shield back into position. His magnificent recovery was marred only by the imperfection of my throw. I had released the axe at the right moment; but unfortunately, my thumb had caught for a moment in the leather thong, deflecting my aim.

Forster, however, had moved to counteract my skill, not my clumsiness. He was quite unprepared when my hard-thrown axe ricocheted off the floor two feet in front of him, rose like a striking cobra and struck upward beneath his guard.

He realized his danger at the last moment and chopped down quickly with his shield. I heard a heavy clang as the rim of the shield struck the axe, and I knew that I was finished.

He stood and grinned at me. Then his shield arm dropped and I saw the axe buried in his chest to the haft. Forster hadn't been quite fast enough to handle my deflection shot; he had managed to hit the handle, but the head was already in him.

Still grinning, he collapsed to the floor. And the room erupted.

25

I had been considering only my own actions. It hadn't occurred to me that Guesci and Karinovsky might be waiting for an opportunity to do something. But they had been ready. And when the axe had buried itself in Forster's chest, they both went into action.

Guesci ran to the weapon-covered wall, and Karinovsky moved in the opposite direction to the serving table beside the fireplace. They began to throw sabres, gin bottles, maces, jars of olives, assegais, cocktail shakers, and the like, catching Forster's men by surprise, and from opposite directions.

Karinovsky was shouting at me, "Get his gun!"

I dived to Forster's side and clawed wildly through his pockets. The guards were firing wildly at the three of us, and I came up with the big automatic and started shooting back. I was partially protected by Forster's body, and I could hear bullets slamming into his back.

"Get back here!" Karinovsky shouted. I looked, and saw him lift a heavy coffee table and throw it across the room. Guesci had ducked down behind the couch. I scrambled to my feet and dove over the couch, landing on my back, out of reach of the bullets.

Then the three of us were behind the couch with one automatic. There were about nine bullets left in the 13-round magazine. Still, if Forster's men had rushed us at once, it would all have been over. But they had gone to cover behind the massive furniture, and now they hesitated, talked it over and decided against a charge.

We had achieved a stalemate. It was not so good as a victory, but it was much better than being killed. Forster's men were 20 feet away from us, concealed behind various chairs and tables. The broad picture window was behind them. We had the couch for protection and the fireplace to our rear. The only way out of the room was by a door to our right. It was in the open, impossible for either side to use.

"What do we do now?" Guesci asked.

I knew the answer to that one. "We wait," I said.

"Could anyone hear the shots in the village?" Karinovsky asked.

Guesci shrugged. "Possibly. But in the off-season, these ski towns have only a single policeman."

"One's better than none," I said. "Maybe he'll help us out."

"And take a chance of being killed?" Guesci

said. "Don't even consider it. At the very most he will contact the regional authorities in Belluno, which is some 50 miles from here. They might conceivably send up a few policemen on the train."

We could hear Forster's men whispering across the room. I said, "Our own people in Villa Santini might take a look."

"I'm sure they will," Karinovsky said. "Eventually. But how long can we wait?"

The whispering had stopped. We heard the creak of a heavy table being manhandled, and I looked quickly around the right side of the couch.

"They're moving up behind the furniture," I said.

Karinovsky nodded his approval. "Movable barricades are an old military device," he told me. "They date back at least to the time of the Greek city-states, and probably earlier."

"What do we do about it?"

"The standard defense is to pour burning oil and molten lead down upon the attackers."

"We'll have to try something else," I said. "Guesci, get back to the other end of the couch. Get ready."

The barricades were about ten feet away. I leaned out and snapped a shot at the nearest table. At that range the nine-millimeter bullet penetrated completely, and the table stopped moving. Guns opened up on the far side of the couch, and I ducked back and flipped the automatic to Guesci.

"One shot," I whispered.

He leaned out and fired. The barricade

stopped on his side. He passed the gun back. An idea occurred to me. I called out, "Your side again, Guesci! Shoot, shoot!" Then I stood up.

At this range, I could see the men lying prone behind the tables. I fired three times, heard a man shout in pain, and then I ducked down again behind the couch.

The barricades had stopped moving. Forster's men were holding another whispered conference. Karinovsky said, "They will rush us this time."

"Perhaps not," Guesci said. "It would be extremely dangerous for them."

"Their alternative," Karinovsky pointed out, "is to let the stalemate continue, which would result in their arrest. Faced with that alternative, they will rush us."

"I think you're right," I said to Karinovsky. "I think we had better act first." I handed him the automatic. "Come on, Guesci."

I crawled backward, away from the couch and toward the fireplace. Guesci followed me, looking dubious about the whole thing. I took off my jacket and wrapped it around my hands, and waited until Guesci had done the same. Then I began pulling branches out of the fire. We pulled and tugged, scorching ourselves liberally. Karinovsky was exchanging shots with the men behind the barricade.

Soon we had a dozen flaming torches in front of us.

"All right," I said. "Try to hit the drapes." We crouched and began to throw. Karinovsky switched to rapid fire.

The drapes were beginning to smoulder, and Forster's men hastily pulled back their barricades. They tore the curtains from the window and started to stamp out the fire.

I had been waiting for that. I took the fire tongs, sprang to my feet like a spearman leaping from ambush, and hurled it at the picture window. It smashed through the center, and we felt the cold mountain wind at once. The fire also felt it; the carpet began to hiss and crackle, and the smouldering drapes were fanned into flame.

We kept on throwing branches and logs, and Karinovsky winged one guard and kept the others distracted. The heavily varnished furniture caught fire, and the flames started to get out of control. Forster's men were caught in an impossible situation. You can't put out a fire in the middle of a gun battle, nor can you keep up your end of a gun battle in the middle of a fire.

Two men broke for the door. Karinovsky winged the first and killed the second. That gave the last man time to dive through the window. Unfortunately for him, he didn't dive high enough. He hung for a moment screaming, impaled on a row of glass daggers, with his hair beginning to burn. Karinovsky emptied the magazine into him.

It was time to get out; a little past time, as a matter of fact. Karinovsky was used up. He got halfway to the door before he collapsed. I tried to lift him, and I couldn't. My left hand refused to take any weight. It was only then that I discovered that at some point in the fighting I had been shot cleanly through the wrist.

Guesci hoisted Karinovsky across his shoulders, and we started again for the door. The room was filled with smoke now, and we blundered into a wall. We felt our way along it, and I had the absurd certainty that we were going to stumble into a closet. I kept on telling Guesci to make sure he found the right door. We kept on walking, and it felt as if we circumnavigated that room three times.

Then my left leg buckled, and I fell down and knew I could never make it to my feet. Guesci stopped, and I shouted at him, "Keep on going!" But he wouldn't go any farther; he was kneeling, laying Karinovsky on the floor beside me.

It was a damned cold fire. Also a wet one.

I thought about that for a while. Then I opened my eyes and looked around. I was lying on wet grass. The lodge, 50 feet behind me, was burning merrily. I wanted to ask Guesci how we had gotten out, and whether Karinovsky was still alive. But I didn't have the strength.

A few seconds later, it seemed to me, we were surrounded by a crowd of villagers. There was a single, embarrassed-looking policeman, and several Americans. I recognized my old buddy, George. And my new buddy, Colonel Baker.

"Nye!" the colonel was saying. "Are you all right? We got here as fast as we could. At first, when we received Guesci's message, we thought—"

I said, in a hard, clear voice, "Your thoughts do not concern me, Colonel. Only your actions, which I find deplorably inefficient."

I was pleased to see Baker look abashed. I had several other choice things to say, but no opportunity to say them. Just about that time I passed out cold.

26

I recovered consciousness in a comfortable bed, in a room overlooking the Alps. But not the Dolomite Alps. A cheerful, middle-aged nurse told me that they were the Carnic Alps. I was in Austria, in the town of Kotschach. More of me seemed to be bandaged than not.

The nurse left, and Colonel Baker came in and brought me up to date.

During the confusion of the fire, Baker and his men had bundled the three of us into a car and driven us across the border with all deliberate speed. This was only expedient; the Italian authorities and press were starting to ask a lot of uncomfortable questions. They would get answers, too; not necessarily true ones, but certainly reasonable ones.

Karinovsky's wounded shoulder had become infected during his strenuous activities. He would have to spend a week or so in a hospital, but would come out none the worse for wear.

Guesci was in a state of nervous collapse. It seemed to be nothing that a few weeks or months on the Riviera wouldn't cure.

They had both given Baker a full account of their activities, as well as mine. Here the Colonel coughed and nervously cleared his throat.

"Frankly, if I did not have the evidence of two witnesses, I could scarcely believe in your exploits. I don't mean to insult you, Nye, but it is *not* very credible. I mean to say—scuba, hydroplane, airplane, a duel with battleaxes—that is hardly the thing one expects of an agent."

"Except," I reminded him, "for a man like Agent X."

"Yes. Very true." The Colonel frowned, pursed his lips, rubbed his cheek with a forefinger, and said, "I want to talk to you about that. I mean, after all, Agent X *was* our invention. But it occurs to me now that I know very little about you. I don't know what you were doing, for example, in the years between your graduation from college and your meeting with George in Paris."

He looked at me hopefully. I smiled and said nothing.

"I don't suppose you'd care to tell me about it?" he asked.

"I prefer not to discuss my past," I said. "But I don't like being referred to as your invention. I think of myself more as your discovery."

"Yes, of course," Baker said. "I thought you might say something like that."

He drummed his fingers on the edge of my bed. I felt no pity for the man. For too long had this junior-grade Father of Lies sat in his web, spinning preposterous dreams for the entrapment of the unwary. Now the illusionist was caught in his own snare. The lie had come home to its master.

"What disturbs me," the Colonel said, "is the possibility that you were never what you seemed to be; that you were, and are, a secret agent of considerable experience; and that you were introduced into the scheme by a different agency of the U.S. government."

"Why would they do that?" I asked.

"In order to spy on us," Baker said unhappily. "Certain agencies have never been willing to accept our autonomous status."

"It sounds farfetched, sir," I told him.

"It does," Baker said. "But then, everything about this case is farfetched. Wouldn't you help us clear up the situation?"

"I have nothing to hide," I said. "And for that reason, I have nothing to say."

"Well," the Colonel said, "perhaps it can't be helped. Uncertainty is our daily diet in the service. The operation has come to a most successful conclusion. You've performed brilliantly, Nye, and I congratulate you. My appreciation, of course, will take more—tangible—forms."

"That's very kind of you, sir."

"Now," Baker said, "I suppose might be a good time to discuss your future."

"My future?"

"Of course. It is not my job to understand the tools at my disposal, only to use them as well as possible. I would like to continue using you, Nye. I would like to put you on full operational duty."

I took my time before answering. I thought of Mavis, now waiting for me in Paris. I thought of the resumption of my life, such as it was. The adventure was over, whether Colonel Baker knew it or not; The Game of X had been played, and could not be played again. It was time for Agent X to exit gracefully, and for William P. Nye to come back to life.

And yet, this reasonable solution dissatisfied me. Like so many of my countrymen, I am shy, friendly, idealistic, and more than a little provincial. Above all, I share in our national preoccupation with exotic danger. Strange lands and mysterious women are never far from my thoughts. My manner is commonplace; but always, as I walk down the matter-of-fact streets of my city, I am listening to waves explode across a coral reef, or wandering through weed-strangled alleys in some lost jungle civilization.

We avoid our true motives, substituting for them a face-saving urgency. I had chosen Baker's money; it had been my apology to the everyday world. By taking it, I could convince myself that I was doing an absurd thing for a practical reason. It was easier to live with than a childhood dream of a watery city.

But now the game was over. Reality, no matter how distasteful, is better than illusion. My curtain speech was brief. I said, "I am sorry, Colonel. It simply isn't possible."

"Think about it for a while," the Colonel said. "Don't come to a decision at once. You would have plenty of time for rest and recuperation. And the question of payment would be easily settled."

I smiled sadly and shook my head.

"And," Colonel Baker said, "we really need you."

"That's very kind of you," I said. "But surely there are other agents?"

"None are suitable for this particular operation. You see, the Celebes have never really been within our operational area; though we once had a man stationed in the Lesser Sunda Islands."

"Hmmm," I said, frowning thoughtfully and trying to remember where the Lesser Sunda Islands were.

"But he's dead," Colonel Baker went on, "and our Sumatra operative disappeared last week in the town of Samarinda in eastern Borneo. He did manage to smuggle out a message with the captain of a Hong Kong junk, who brought it to our weather station in the Sulu Archipelago."

"Yes, yes, I see," I said, seeing nothing but feeling a vast temptation rise within me. I had never been to the Orient. My only experience with the mysterious East was some evenings spent in the tortuous streets of New York's Chinatown. And, of course, I had seen many movies, and had read innumerable books. . . .

I pulled myself together with an effort. "You're going a little too fast for me, sir," I said to Colonel Baker. "I mean, why, specifically would you need me?"

"We have no other agent who speaks fluent Tagalog as well as Yunnanese," the Colonel replied.

I stared at him. Who, I wondered, had been scribbling in my dossier? Where was my lie taking me? As a matter of fact—could I be sure that it *was* a lie? Might I not actually be Agent X, suffering from a minor lapse of memory? It seemed as reasonable as the farfetched notion that I was actually William Nye.

"It also helps," the Colonel said, "that you are able to sail a *prau.*"

I nodded automatically. Then, with great firmness, I said, "No! I can't do it and that's final!"

"Think it over," Colonel Baker said.

He left the room then, well content with the damage he had done. I leaned back in my bed and told myself to be sensible. But I could feel the spell of the East begging me to return to its shallow sunlit seas, its indolent cities, its villages, where a spiritual fatigue erupts periodically into unreasoning passion. And I smelled again the cloying spices, the sharp scent of kerosene and charcoal, and the decay that creeps out of the dim jungles and rots men and their ideas. . . .

Why, after all, did I have to live with reality? Wasn't illusion a perfectly suitable condition?